THERE WAS ONLY ONE MAN TOUGH ENOUGH TO WEAR

POSEY'S SPURS

BY HOWARD E. GREAGER

Author
Howard E. Greager

WESTERN REFLECTIONS, INC.

Ouray, Colorado

This book is respectfully dedicated to the preservation of true western history and the people who lived it.

First Edition

Copyright ©1999 Howard E. Greager
All rights reserved including the right of reproduction in whole or in part.

ISBN 1-890437-30-1

Library of Congress Catalog Number:
99-61616

Western Reflections, Inc.
P. O. Box 710
Ouray, Colorado 81427

Cover art by Phyllis Walker
Interior design by Laurie Goralka Design

Table of Contents

BOOK ONE
The Life and Times of "Mancos Jim" Stephens 1

BOOK TWO
The McDaniels Brothers and the Westfall/Dunlap Murders 67

BOOK THREE
The Buried Treasure of the McCarty Gang 111

BOOK FOUR
A Mysterious Death in Gypsum Valley 133

BOOK FIVE
A Cancer in His Gut — Honey Dunham's Revenge 147

BOOK SIX
Murder Along the Fenceline 155

BOOK SEVEN
A Day in the Life of a Cowboy 161

About the Author 166

Expanded Bibliography 168

Index 170

BOOK ONE:
The Life and Times of "Mancos Jim" Stephens

Introduction

¶ The following true story is a tale of southwest Colorado history as it is remembered by some of the people who lived it. It is a tale of a young boy who was raised by his gambler father after the family's older children had already grown up and left home.

Gamblers were a breed apart and many were given over to strong drink. Why, I'm not sure. Intoxication breeds recklessness and that is not a good trait for a gambler. I'm quite sure that the sober gamblers were the most consistent winners. As I speak of gamblers I am not referring to the professionals who traveled from town to town, on a regular circuit, and fleeced the local townspeople. I mean the everyday working man who had developed a craze for it and couldn't pass up a chance to sit in on a game of chance. Any family that had a gambler as the head of the household was destined to suffer many hardships. His absence from home was the biggest loss to the family. His guidance and care for the family members was an irreplaceable asset to the proper upbringing of his children. Any child of a gambler father who grew to adulthood and became a respectable citizen of some worth was more of a credit to him or herself than to anyone else.

High stakes gamblers, if they were consistent winners, were sometimes called for cheating with a marked deck or other devices they used to know what cards the other players were holding. When this event took place, the winning gambler might have to defend his life with whatever weapon he preferred to use. A small caliber pistol such as the two shot Derringer was the preferred one but knives were in common use also. Some gamblers, of great strength and agility, used pressure points of the human body to render a protester instantly and utterly helpless.

The gambler who is the main character in the story that follows used the "pressure point" technique to subdue any objectors to his methods of winning at cards or any other physical confrontation. He came to be known as a very tough person. His reputation spread as a person that you should leave alone for reasons of your personal health. My own father knew him well and I remember hearing him say that when "Mancos Jim" walked into a saloon where there were people drinking at the bar, and said he was having a drink on them, he was served first and fast. No one objected. If on a rare occasion when some newcomer to the area, who had never heard of Mancos Jim and didn't feel like paying for his drink, spoke up, he was promptly introduced to a quick grab and twist of the wrist — a sure fire cure. That was Mancos Jim's favorite pressure point and he proved it very effective. At the age of seventy three he tried to use that maneuver again (and for the last time in his life) to try to save himself from the humiliation of being jailed by an over-zealous young night marshal who was trying to put him in the "calaboose" for alleged drunkenness.

Gamblers' wives were left, for the most part, to shift for themselves. If they had children it fell their lot to be the main provider and counselor. Many of them operated home laundries and did ironing, sewing and housework for other people. Some might operate a small cafe or perhaps a "flop house" where persons needing a place to sleep could unroll their blankets. A few, of looser morals and not burdened with children, became madams of bordellos and worked in the saloons in conjunction with their gambler husbands.

A person would almost have to know a gambler personally to be able to understand why they would leave their families and the comforts of home life to prefer sitting at a card table amidst clouds of tobacco smoke, ashtrays with their stinking cigar butts and spittoons reeking with the residue of plug chewing patrons whether they were players or bystanders. The answer is the thrill of gambling and winning. To find money is a grand feeling. Winning at gambling is akin to this — to be able to go home with a pocket full of money and the feeling of having beaten the odds. When the gambler had to go home a loser, his attitude more often than not was tempered with a few drinks of "booze," and would be one of indifference.

This author has personally known several gamblers who were so dedicated to cards and whiskey that they would spend every dime they could get their hands on at the saloon gaming tables. They couldn't even be trusted to be asked to go to town for badly needed groceries because, with a few dollars in their pocket, their lust for gambling would dominate all other senses. They all lost their families, their homes, their jobs and their ability to remain in the work force. They couldn't be depended upon for anything, if they had money to gamble with — this perhaps earned from a few months of summer work that was available to them because there were no other workers at that time. They all died in the poor house and were buried in a potter's field. Even as late as today I am in contact with both men and women who are looking for information about their fathers, who had been divorced because of gambling when the children were too small to remember them.

Let us now begin the true story of Mancos Jim Stephens: a cowboy, rancher, teamster, miner, timberman, and rough and tumble saloon fighter. Last but not least, he was a gambler whose burning desire dominated all other aspects of his exciting and colorful life. The story is a biography of Mancos Jim (James F.) Stephens, combined with events as seen by Thomas Lloyd Stephens, youngest child of James F. Stephens and Josephine Amanda Exon Stephens.

"I am a roving gambler, I've gambled all around,
Whenever I meet with a deck of cards, I lay my money down."

1: The Early Years

James F. Stephens was born in Little Rock, Arkansas, on December 6, 1866, to Ely Hiram Stephens and Nancy Catherine Sargent Stephens. He was called Jim almost from birth and grew up with a half-brother, William, in bog and squirrel country. He had a sister who married a Dr. Kent from Kent, Texas. Jim had a certain amount of schooling. Back in those days a boy was old enough to do a day's work at age twelve and that was generally the end of their school experience. By age fourteen, from working at various jobs, Jim acquired a gray mare and a saddle and left the cane breaks of Arkansas to see what the world had to offer.

Jim roamed around the country for several years, working here and there at different jobs. He learned how to drive plodding teams of oxen and haul freight. He tried livery stable work but did not care to spend that much time around the awful stink of the stalls that had to be cleaned regularly. Once again he was on the move and his travels eventually took him to the vast cattle ranges of West Texas. He was desperately in need of a job and offered his services to every possible employer. Nothing was to be had in the way of employment and it wasn't long before he had to sell the mare and saddle for money to eat on. In desperation he entered a saloon in Abilene, Texas, where he had noticed a number of saddled horses tied at the hitch rail. All bore the same brand which was known all over the country as the Hash Knife outfit. Inside, the bartender told him that one of the players at the card table was the foreman of the Aztec Cattle & Land Co., who were the owners of the Hash Knife brand. Jim approached the table and along with a few other spectators was watching the play of the cards. In his innocent approach to the table, Jim hadn't noticed that he had stopped directly behind the chair of a man with half of one ear gone.

In the early days of the West it wasn't uncommon to see a person with some body part missing. Missing fingers were common on cowboys from getting them caught in the dallies on a saddle horn. After roping something, generally cattle, the cowboy's end of the rope was wrapped around the saddle horn to bring the animal to a stop. If fingers were caught in the wraps (dallies) the thousand or so pounds on the end of the rope, bucking and bawling to get loose, would crush the fingers so badly that they would have to be taken off. Also if a person had been shot at, a very close miss could result in part of an ear gone or a bad scar along some part of the face.

In a short while the card player with part of his ear missing turned to Jim and asked him to move. There was always the possibility of an accomplice flashing signals to a player in the game pertaining to the cards held by the person he was standing behind. All gamblers were very touchy about this rule of spectators standing back far enough that they couldn't read any of the player's cards. There were people who thought "Wild Bill" Hickok was a little strange because he would never tolerate anyone behind his back whether he was playing cards or not. The one time that he forgot to enforce this rule, he was killed by a bullet from a gun held by a man with a grudge who had slipped behind his back.

Jim didn't know the rules that the card players had concerning where he was standing. He was definitely not a friend of anyone there and had intended no harm to anyone. He didn't heed the warning. A bit later the half-eared cowboy slid quickly from his chair and made a grab for his holstered .45. As Jim had no gun, and not knowing what else to do, he jumped right up against the man, so close that he couldn't draw the gun. The cowboy, realizing that he was about to shoot an unarmed man, for which he could be hanged, took off the gun belt and laid it on the card table. He rather offhandedly remarked to the crowd that he would teach this young whelp a few things about spectator etiquette at a card table. The crowd formed a ring around the combatants and the fight was on.

From the start it didn't look like a fair match-up. Even at nineteen years of age, Jim Stephens weighed close to a hundred and ninety pounds and was tall for his age — nearing six feet. His adversary, who was called "Crop" by his friends, was only about five feet nine inches tall and probably didn't weigh over a hundred and forty pounds soaking wet. After a little sparring and the exchange of a few light blows, Jim made a lightning quick grab of the man's arm when he missed with a punch aimed at Jim's head. To get hold of the arm was the important part. Next thing to do was get the wrist-hand area and find the nerve, and after the proper pressure was applied, the man would be reduced to helplessness but not really hurt. Jim had learned this trick from a freighter in East Texas he worked for who claimed he learned it from an Osage Indian.

When tempers quieted some, Jim asked who the foreman was

of the Hash Knife outfit. Crop, the other man in the fight with him, replied, "I am." Jim said, "I am looking for a job." Crop then replied, "Well, young fellow, I would rather have you on my side, than against me. Consider yourself hired. We have bought a herd of cattle from the Continental Cattle and Land Company of Abilene, Texas, and are trailing them to northern Arizona. Pick five head of saddle horses for your string out of the remuda tomorrow." The card game abruptly ended and the cowboys all left the saloon. As Jim passed by the bartender, he heard the remark, "Hell of a note that you have to whip the foreman to get a job."

2: *The Hash Knife*

The cattle in this first drive numbered about 6,500 head and started on the trail in May of 1885. Two drives were made that year totaling 11,600 head delivered in Arizona. They were driven on a route up the Pecos River into New Mexico near Fort Sumner and then turned west towards the Rio Grande, crossing it at Isleta a few miles below Albuquerque. From there it was nearly a straight line northwest to Holbrook, Arizona, where, at the junction of the Rio Puerco and the Little Colorado Rivers, headquarters had been established. It required about sixty days to walk the cattle the 600 miles to Arizona. They arrived there in better condition than when they left Texas.

Those hauled by rail, in later years, suffered greatly and were in very poor shape upon arrival and required several weeks to regain the lost weight from the shipping. The cattle hauled in on the railroad also had to be delivered to Winslow, at extra cost, as there were inadequate unloading facilities at Holbrook. So the trail drives continued for many years. Some herds were driven about halfway and then loaded onto a train for delivery over the last half of the route. In all, over 37,000 head of Texas cattle were moved from the range in West Texas to the range in northern Arizona. Added to this total were approximately 16,000 steers that went north to the area around Miles City, Montana. All of these cattle were owned by The Aztec Cattle & Land Company.

That is one thing that Texas had a lot of — cattle, cattle and more cattle. There were so many, in fact, that during the terrible winter of 1887 it was said that a person could walk across the panhandle of Texas on the bodies of dead cattle. There must have been some exciting times during those drives. They had to go right by the ranch of Clay Allison who was a notorious gunman and member of the Stockton Gang. All of northern New Mexico was a nest of cattle rustlers and outlaws as well as a haven for desperados wanted in Texas for various crimes. Also, the many Indian tribes of northern Arizona demanded a certain number of cattle as payment for crossing their lands.

Jim worked for the Hash Knife outfit until the trail drive reached Holbrook, Arizona, and for a considerable time afterwards. He and Crop became good friends and most of their spare time was spent teaching Jim the finer points of gambling with a deck of cards. Crop had been at it for many years and he was a very clever card player. Jim was a good learner and for the rest of his life he was a slave to the rattle of chips, the silky riffle of a deck of cards and the beckoning green cloth of a card table. Like all gamblers, when his luck was good, he had money in every pocket. But when he was broke, he was so broke, he couldn't buy a cup of coffee. This taught Jim a valuable lesson and that was not to lose every cent he had. He had to set a limit to lose. That way he could eat for a few days.

This part of Arizona was a cattleman's paradise until about 1900 when it began to be grazed out. Before 1900, grass belly high to a cow was everywhere as far as the eye could see and the cattlemen took full advantage of the free food with their herds numbering in the tens of thousands. During roundup time there was a lot of night herding to be done to keep the steers cut from the herd to be shipped for beef from re-entering the herd that was to be turned back to the range. Night time was when the cowboys did their singing in hopes that a soothing sound would help the cattle to bed down and be less agitated and likely to spook at something. Cowboys made up their own verses to fit what ever mood either they or the cattle were in. It is interesting to know that the first four verses of the song "Cowboy Heaven," were first sung by a half-Indian cowboy from Utah while night herding on the Hash Knife cattle range of northern Arizona.

"Last night as I lay on the prairie and
gazed at the stars in the sky,
I wondered if ever a cowboy could drift to
that sweet bye and bye."

3: A Cowboy

The Aztec Cattle & Land Co., alias Hash Knife, had bought over 1,000,000 acres of land in northeastern Arizona from the A & P Railroad. It stretched from Holbrook west to Winslow, and a part of the range went west nearly to Flagstaff. The southern boundary was the Mogollon Rim. All of this range was already well stocked with cattle. Several outfits like the "24" were nearly as large as the Aztec and several large bands of sheep were grazing there before the Hash Knife cattle arrived. The Aztec herds filled the range to capacity. The railroad was very slow in presenting Aztec with the deeds to the land they had bought and this gave people seeking home sites an opening to get settled on the Hash Knife range. In order to keep "squatters" off the land, they hired a number of renegade Texas gunmen to enforce their wishes. After the people had been forced to "pack up and move out," most of their cattle remained on the Hash Knife range.

This brazen gang soon got the idea to gather and ship them to market after rebranding was taken care of. After awhile the rebranding was forsaken and the cattle were shipped under the brands they wore. The proceeds from the sale would go to the shipper and the rustlers knew full well the owners would be too afraid of them to demand their money. This was so easy that they eventually turned on their employers and started mixing Hash Knife and other cattle with the herds they gathered from the people forced to leave the country. Winslow was the shipping point for as many as

2,000 head of stolen cattle a month. The rustler gang was making close to 100% profit as they were riding Hash Knife horses, feeding them Hash Knife grain and they were all on the Hash Knife payroll. With well over 1,000,000 acres of land to hide in, and probably 100,000 head of cattle to maverick from, it's small wonder that the rustling business was so lucrative. Brand inspection at the shipping point was practically non-existent.

These men are typical of the Hash Knife cowboys. Hank Sharp is the third from the left in the front row.
Courtesy of Richard & Virginia Rogers

Zane Gray, in his book "The Hash Knife Outfit," tells of a gambler he called Carr and a "young kid" who was never referred to by name. When the irate cattlemen from northern Arizona finally wiped out the Hash Knife cattle rustlers the only survivors were Jed Stone the foreman, and the "kid" who had rolled his "soogans," loaded a pack horse and pulled out for the Tonto Basin just one day ahead of the big fight. Stone had insisted that the kid get away and not stay there, through some boyhood sense of loyalty, and be killed. Stone had been warned of what was going to happen by a cattleman's daughter, who was in love with him. Just before the big fight many of the Hash Knife rustlers, through gambling and drunken distrust of each other, were destroyed from within. When the posse of cattlemen arrived at the headquarter's cabin of the Hash Knife cattle rustlers all they found was a burned cabin, several corpses scorched beyond recognition and other bodies scattered about in the pines surrounding the cabin. Their leader and boss had escaped.

During these years Jim Stephens was exposed to every kind of outlaw that worked for the Hash Knife outfit. One cowboy who worked for the Hash Knife had been asked to leave southwestern Colorado because he had started two Indian wars, shot at least two Indians, and his presence was no longer desired there. He packed his "hot roll" and in a few days riding was on the cattle ranges of northeastern Arizona. His name was Hank Sharp and he made quite a name for himself as a cowboy in the White Mountains and other places. Jim spent time studying these men, learning their habits, all their little idiosyncrasies and in general what made them "tick." In his later years Jim would find this knowledge very useful when he was called upon to track down cattle rustlers and other criminals. He did it with such expertise and dispatch one would think him trained in that profession.

Hank Sharp as he appeareed when he first arrived in Apache County, Arizona, where he served as a deputy sheriff for a while.
Courtesy of Richard & Virginia Rogers

"Crop" may have been the gambler Zane Grey referred to as "Carr," and Jim Stephens may have been "the kid." Jim stayed among the stockmen of the Tonto Basin, buying and selling horses. He never sided with the Tewksburys or the Grahams in their feud to control the Tonto Basin. He was an innocent observer of the sheep and cattle war that all but ruined the Tonto

Basin range and the people who had settled there. He was there when Sheriff Commodore Owens shot little Sam Houston Blevins, aged ten, when he jumped out of a ranch house window to go for help and then died in his mother's arms. Jim lived among the Spanish people for awhile and learned the language. He acquired a matched pair of .45's. Later in Tucson, Arizona, a gunsmith converted them to .38 caliber on the same frames.

4: Mancos Jim

About 1888 Jim Stephens migrated to southwestern Colorado and went into the cattle business, registering the Hash Knife brand in Colorado. He used it there for quite a few years and when he let it go the brand was recorded in the name of John Verdi Hotchkiss who in later years was the brand inspector for Montrose and Delta Counties and adjacent areas. Jim arrived in Durango, Colorado in time to witness the hanging of a bank robber from Kansas. The bank robber had ridden the train into Durango (Animas City as it was called then) and made his way over Wolf Creek Pass into the San Luis Valley but was so hotly pursued by investigators that he stole a pack mule and made his way back across Wolf Creek Pass and into Durango where he was caught still in possession of the stolen money. An angry crowd hanged him near the present location of the high school.

Before the coming of the railroad to Silverton in 1882 all the freight for the town and the hundreds of working mines was hauled in by freight wagons pulled by long strings of ox teams. Shortly after Jim's arrival in Durango, because of his experience freighting with ox teams, he was offered the contract to skid a steam boiler to Silverton, where it would probably be used for a sawmill or crushing plant. Why it wasn't brought in on the railroad remains a mystery. Possibly it was too large for some of the tunnels. The skidding operation was accomplished with forty head of oxen and must have taken close to a month. The only route to follow was a rough trail made previously by teamsters with their wagons and many strings of pack mules and burros.

After getting the steam boiler to its destination Jim began looking for work whereby he could use the oxen. He heard of a road construction job at Schofield Pass and transported the pairs of oxen. He worked there until the road was completed to the town of Marble, Colorado, where a huge deposit of very nice marble was being quarried. The year was probably 1890. Jim stayed around for awhile and built several houses for the workers at the quarry. About 1891 he moved his oxen teams to Montrose and sold them to Dave Wood who needed every kind of draft animal he could get to pull the freight wagons bound for the mines of Telluride, Rico and Ouray.

Very shortly after this Jim was back in southwestern Colorado and took a job with a man named Jim Caviness who had cattle in the general area of the top of Mancos Hill and a considerable portion of Lost Canyon. Caviness had two teen-aged sons but he trusted Jim with the riding and looking after the cattle. Caviness had trouble saddling and mounting a horse because of a crippled arm he had received in a logging accident. Of course Jim couldn't see all of the range every day and Caviness helped out when necessary. The Lost Canyon range had been left unattended for several days and Caviness made a ride down there to see how things were. Caviness had some very strong suspicions that a man named John McGooch was stealing cattle from him. Too many times he had seen fresh branded calves in McGooch's corral with no mothers for them anywhere around. That type of cattle raising is difficult to explain. Caviness promptly discovered about fifty heifers with calves were missing. This wasn't McGooch's style. He would never be that bold. This was the work of experienced cattle rustlers.

Caviness found the trail where the cattle had been driven out of the canyon area and by their tracks it looked like the rustlers might be heading them in the direction of Red Mesa and the New Mexico state line. He quickly made his way back to the ranch and informed Jim of what he had found and asked him if he would take their trail and see if he could get the stolen cattle back. The brand they all wore was the Rocking C. Caviness allowed his two sons to go along. He felt sure that Jim would take care of them.

Ten days later they arrived back at the ranch with the fifty head of cows and calves. The animals were in very poor condition from so much trailing and not having time to stop and fill their bellies. The rustlers had moved them at a very fast pace.

Jim and the boys had benefited quite well from their adventure as they had acquired twelve extra horses, three with saddles and several guns. I don't know what the fate of the cattle rustlers was. The unwritten law of the land was that horse thieves and cattle rustlers were hanged when caught red handed plying their trade. For years afterwards the cattle rustlers made a wide circle around the range of Jim Caviness. As a bonus for a job well done Caviness gave Jim Stephens a two-year-old sorrel, blaze-faced stud colt. Jim kept the colt awhile, long enough to get him broke to saddle and ride and then he sold him to Fred Haller of Hallersville just west of Mancos. Haller made a racehorse out of the colt and named him Silver Dick. He became famous in that part of the country and made quite a bit of money for the Haller family.

Not long after the stolen heifers incident, Caviness was in Mancos and walked into one of the saloons. John McGooch was seated at a card table with a bottle of "booze," having a few drinks. Caviness only cast a quick glance in that direction and walked to the bar, not having spoken a word to anyone, and ordered a couple of "whiskies." After finishing the drinks he stood there in thoughtful meditation. Apparently he was going over in his mind exactly what he was going to do. He started for the door but upon reaching it he drew his six-gun, and in that famous old Texas gunfighter style of walk away, whirl and shoot, he fired five bullets into the body of McGooch, who was dead before his body hit the floor. Caviness calmly walked across the street, reloading his pistol as he went, mounted his horse and rode out of town. Afterwards he was sentenced to serve fifteen years in prison and that was the end of Jim Stephen's employment with Jim Caviness.

About this time in Jim's life he became known as "Mancos Jim" with somewhat of a reputation as a man hunter and Jim Caviness's right hand man. He also met his future wife, the youngest daughter of William James Exon.

The Exon family Coat of Arms as documented in Burke's General Armory.
Courtesy of Lorelei Stephens Sutherland

5: *Mancos Jim Marries*

William James Exon was born in Dover, England, one of five brothers who migrated to the United States. Their father, Somrial Exon, was a king's guard which may have entitled the family to own a coat of arms. After their arrival in America the boys split up, with William going to Kansas Territory. Here he married Katorce Dix on January 23, 1859, settled on Rock Creek, Kansas Territory, and raised their family. Like so many others of that time they were hearing stories of the vast amount of land available farther west, how easy it was to obtain and the multitude of opportunities that went with it. They loaded several wagons with all the kids and all the household goods they could carry and started the overland trek to the Mancos Valley of southwestern Colorado.

The first settlers into the valley had to let their wagons down Mancos Hill with rope, block and tackle. After a few years there was a sort of trail that wagons could negotiate by the very careful handling of the teams by the drivers. Well behaved horses and oxen were very important to the progress of the pioneers. In a few years' time a fort was built in the valley as protection from the all-too-frequent Indian raids.

Six and eight horse teams were commonly seen pulling freight wagons into the Mancos Valley.

Courtesy of Joe Walters

By 1881 the Exon children were beginning to marry into the other families of the valley. Sarah Anne married Martin Rush. Minnie Exon married a man named Cramer. John Exon, the oldest boy, married Bell Anne Thornell in 1884. Mary Elizabeth Exon married Charles Eamont Delameter in 1881. Salmon (Sol) Samile Exon married Katie Doramer Parker in 1884. William James Exon II married Ida Broadhead in 1899. Jeorge Exon, the youngest boy, married Grace Bower. Josephine Amanda Exon, the youngest girl, married James F. Stephens (Mancos Jim) in 1892. Martin Rush, along with the Wetherills, was given credit for the discovery of Spruce Tree House on the Mesa Verde. The Wetherills were traders with the Navajo along with their cattle ranching. The Exons were ranchers, sheep men, shingle mill operators, miners, merchants, gamblers and cattlemen. All were good law abiding and respected citizens. William (Bill) Exon built a mercantile store in the town of Dolores, Colorado, which still stands today as a museum.

A short while after Mancos Jim married he was called upon to go down into the Four Corners area to try to apprehend an Indian renegade who had been causing a lot of trouble, not only on the reservation of the Navajos but to the white settlers who lived there. It was believed that he was the same Indian who shot and killed Amasa Barton at his trading post on the San Juan River below Bluff, Utah, in 1887. The Navajos called him "The Bully." They left him strictly alone and they would have nothing to do with him. They secretly wanted to see him taken into custody because he stole their horses, killed their sheep, slept with their wives and made himself at home in any of their hogans whether he was invited in or not. He was very mean to everyone, and came and went, plundering whatever he pleased.

Because of the success he had with the Caviness cattle rustlers and other experiences with outlaws, Mancos Jim seemed like a good choice for the job of going after this bad Indian. He was a friend of all the local tribes and spoke Ute and Navajo. He was well liked by the Indians and could count on help from them to fulfill his mission. Also, Jim was a brother-in-law to Martin Rush who was involved in a partnership with the Wetherills. They ran a trading post in the Four Corners area and could also be a source of information and help when needed. Jim Stephens started on his journey to the Four Corners and not long after his arrival at the Wetherill's trading post several Navajo sheepmen came forward with information as to where the Indian badman could be found.

This bad Indian had a number of hiding places to which he fled when trouble loomed on the horizon. He had been pursued by soldiers on several occasions and had always escaped them leaving numerous casualties among their ranks. In a few days Mancos Jim was in the vicinity of one of the hideouts used by The Bully. From several of his vantage points the renegade could easily see that someone was following his trail. He scoffed at the thought of one man being foolish enough to ride his trail with thoughts of apprehending him. He began to lay plans for an ambush by doubling back on his trail and was especially careful to make the trail very difficult to follow.

Mancos Jim was just as good at following the trail and by accurately assessing the Indian's next moves soon had the outlaw cornered in the rocks where there was no escape. When Jim had worked his way within easy talking distance he yelled to the outlaw in his native tongue and told him he was going to take him in to the jailhouse. The Bully answered him with a fusillade of shots, and said that he didn't like the jail and would never be taken there alive. He still expected to be victorious when the six-shooter showdown arrived. He was counting on a face-to-face shoot out. No one he had ever known or heard of had the audacity to follow him into his own stronghold, corner him into a defensive position and then have the nerve to talk about taking him to the jailhouse.

During the night Jim was able to gain a more favorable position to shoot from and when it was daylight enough to see clearly he put a bullet into the body of the outlaw. The Bully was badly hit and instinct told him he could not survive such a wound. The Angel of Death was hovering above him and already the icy fingers were clutching at his heart. He called to Jim to come to him as he had something he wanted to say. Jim very cautiously made his way to the wounded man, fully expecting an "old Indian trick," and made his presence known. The Bully started talking. He said he had a pair of silver and turquoise spurs that were made for him by Chief Posey of the Paiutes whom he considered to be the toughest man alive. He then told Jim that he was a very brave man to try to take him in by himself as he had killed and wounded several others, including soldiers, who had previously tried. Indians admire bravery in a person regardless of their color or background. As the Indian was dying he handed the spurs to Mancos Jim with these words: "Take them, Mancos Jim. They are yours. I give them to the only man tough enough to wear *"Posey's Spurs."*

6: Children Come

Walter Stephens was the first child born to Jim and Josephine Amanda, January 2, 1893. Two years later, on April 25,1895, their second son, Albert, was born. A third child, a daughter they named Eva, was born in 1897. Shortly after the year 1900 a son they named Jim was born, and about 1901, their second daughter, Frances, was born. Then in 1913, at the age of thirty six, Amanda gave birth to another girl they named Catherine Katorce. More surprises were on the way as Thomas Lloyd was born in 1916 when Amanda was thirty-nine and Jim was fifty. With four boys and three girls, the strain was really beginning to show on Amanda.

Jim always got quite a chuckle telling about his oldest son Walter, at age five, getting his tongue stuck on a stove lid one real frosty morning. The old stove sat outside by the kitchen door and the heavy coating of frost looked good enough to eat and Walter was going to lick up some of it. The first lick, his tongue was stuck fast and he jerked free leaving the skin from the end of his tongue with the lid. He let out a yell of pain and ran crying into the house. While Jim and Amanda were trying to comfort and doctor him, Albert, two years younger than Walter, slipped unnoticed from his chair and went out to the stove and did the very same thing. Only he was smarter than his big brother. When he felt his tongue was stuck he picked up the stove lid and carried it into the house where a little warming freed his tongue. Walter had a sore tongue for a few days.

After Walter was grown and had left home he worked for his uncle Bill Exon in Dolores where Bill operated a butcher shop. Walter learned the trade of butchering from him and then ventured out into the world on his own. He found a job working at the butcher trade in the town of Delta, Colorado. He found a wife there and they started a family. Mancos Jim was away working in the mines and Amanda wanted to go to Delta to see her oldest son. There was only one way to do it. She packed food and clothing into the buggy, hitched up the team and proceeded to make the trip. It was more than likely a five-day trip as it would have been over a hundred miles by the shortest possible route. The trip was a terrible strain on her as she had with her a three-year old girl and her youngest son, one-year-old Thomas Lloyd. After he grew to manhood he was known by his middle name, Lloyd, all over southwestern Colorado.

Mancos Jim and his wife "Josie" are shown here with five of their children. Tom and Catherine were not yet born. Left to right in the back row are Walter, Eva and Albert. Left to right in the front row is Francis, Mancos Jim, Josie and Jim, Jr.
Courtesy of Lorelei Stephens Sutherland

Mancos Jim could speak the Ute tongue pretty well and also the Spanish language. He treated the Utes fairly when he had dealings with them and they respected him for it. There was a Paiute Chief who lived in Allen Canyon on the east side of Elk Mountain who also was known by the name of Mancos Jim. The Utes and Paiutes collected names for themselves from any person they admired.

For example, the Paiute Chief, Sawagerie, liked and admired a cowboy by the name of Bill Posey who worked for the Carlisle Cattle Company. Bill was a Texas cowboy and dressed well. He was probably admired by a lot more people than just the Paiute chief. This chief adopted the name of "Posey" for himself. Hundreds of these Indians had taken the white man's names. It is not known for sure but it seems likely that the Paiute in Allen Canyon liked and admired Mancos Jim and adopted his name to himself. But it is also entirely possible that there just happened to be two people in the same general area with the same name. Mancos Jim had the respect of the Utes and that respect was later on to be a very useful tool for him.

7: Amanda Dies

In the spring of 1913 Jim Stephens and a partner named Frink trailed 800 head of Utah cattle to the 850-acre Fred Taylor ranch, near Mancos, which they had bought. They then had fifteen head of purebred Hereford bulls shipped in to build up the quality of the cattle. Later the partners bought 100 acres on Mesa Verde from Fred Armstrong. To go with this purchase they bought 100 head of cattle that also had grazing rights on Mesa Verde. A later purchase of 300 head of cattle from the Hepworth Brothers completed their ranch requirements. This partnership was being developed on a broad, firm basis. Jim Stephens was the ranch manager. He was well on his way to being a respected and useful member of the Mancos community. After a few years the partnership was dissolved, perhaps because of Jim's love of gambling, and Jim went to a ranch at the mouth of Webber Canyon.

Mancos Jim farmed in a modest way, enough to keep riding stock and a few work horses on the place. He did lots of work for other people and kept his kids in shoes and overalls. In winter he usually cut ties for the railroad. Jim's former working partner from the days in Schofield Pass, Taylor Norton, came to Mancos and together they worked the timber to get out the much needed ties. Men who could do this work were in great demand by the railroads as they never had enough ties to lay their ever expanding rail systems on.

In 1916, Mancos Jim was working at the Sunnyside Mill near Silverton, Colorado, and due to the distance to travel (over eighty-five miles) it was not considered economical to try to get home on weekends to visit the family. Very few workers tried it unless they were close to home. It was a full day's travel one way from Mancos to Silverton. The usual routine was for the worker to stay three months at a time and then go home for perhaps a week or so before coming back to work. Some of the miners, if they only intended to work through the winter months, would stay the full time and then return to their farms for the summer. This was the way Mancos Jim tried to do it.

When he returned home early that summer Aunt Belle Exon showed him a clipping from the Mancos newspaper. It read: "While Josephine (Amanda) Stephens was taking in washing to support herself and two children, Mancos Jim was gambling away his wages and spending his free time in the 'red light' district of Silverton." Jim was furious over the article and saddled up the two horses for a ride into town. His ranch was twelve miles out of Mancos. Amanda rode side saddle and had the diaper bag (for Lloyd) hanging from the side. Lloyd rode on a pillow in front of Jim and they proceeded into town. Jim rode right up to the front of the newspaper office as the owner was coming down the street from the post office.

When the editor had almost reached the door Jim cut him off with his horse and handed him the newspaper clipping. After the editor looked the clipping over, Mancos Jim said, "Eat it." He backed his horse slightly so his hand could easily reach the diaper bag. After a short hesitation, the printer, who shall remain anonymous, put the paper in his mouth, chewed it up and swallowed it. Jim never did say if he had a pistol in the diaper bag or not, or, if he would have used it. Anyhow the effect was the same. Jim's reputation as a tough customer got a boost.

Lloyd was barely a year old when Amanda died in 1917. A doctor pulled all of her teeth at the same time because they were all ulcerated in the roots. The huge amount of poison that drained into her system was more than her heart could stand. Death was attributed to blood poisoning. She is buried in the Mancos cemetery in one of two graves that were won in a poker game by Mancos Jim.

The children's aunt, Audie Cramer, took care of Catherine and Lloyd for awhile. Then, their sister Frances, barely sixteen, took them to Antonito on the border of New Mexico. Jim had a job there, once again cutting ties for the Denver and Rio Grande Railroad. It seemed like sister Frances dragged Catherine and Lloyd all over southern Colorado. She was a waitress and worked wherever she could find a job. Eventually, she returned to familiar country and got a job waiting tables in a cafe at a place near Telluride called Vance Junction. Catherine and Lloyd were left in care of their second-oldest brother, Albert, who lived and worked in Telluride. (The story of his days in that boom town was published in the magazine section of The Grand Junction Sentinel, Nov. 10, 1974, by its Norwood correspondent, Grace Herndon.)

8: Jim Remarries

Jim later returned to the Mancos area and before long he made the acquaintance of a woman named Ella Selack. She was the cook at the Mandarin Cafe in Durango. They were soon married and that same year Jim went into a partnership with three other men in a cattle and ranching venture. They were Frank Stevens, Elliott Megaliard, and Clarence Teague. They leased a ranch at the mouth of Webber Creek where it runs into the Mancos River. They also leased the southwestern Colorado grazing rights from the Ute Indians and had summer pasture in the area of the Tipown Dam above Mancos. That gave them a pretty complete outfit: winter range, summer range and a hay ranch to grow feed for the necessary extra feeding of late calving and old or weak livestock. Mancos Jim was the one who ran the hay ranch. For the first time since Lloyd was one year old, he had a place to live that might be permanent — no more being dragged around by his job hunting sister.

Here Lloyd came into his first memories of his stepmother hollering at him. He was rummaging around in an old dump and found a cast iron bank in the shape of a camel. It had one leg broken off and would not stand without being propped up. It was dirty and rusty but he was mighty proud of it. It was the first toy Lloyd ever had and finding it made it more of a treasure. Ella threw it out — she said it was too dirty. Lloyd doesn't remember being a bad boy but remembers that he sure got hollered at a lot. It seems like she was always hollering about something. "Lloyd, wash your hands. Lloyd, get the wood in. Lloyd, dry the dishes for Catherine. Lloyd, don't you ever make your bed?" But her cooking was wonderful — wonderful hot biscuits and homemade jelly from wild plums, or a nice thick heel of fresh-baked bread on the plate with gobs of fresh churned butter.

Lloyd was a big six-year-old when one of Megaliard's foremen started to teach him what was to be done as the horse wrangler at round-up time. He had to get up way before daylight, saddle up the night horse that was kept on a picket rope, and find the horse remuda grazing out on the open range. This really was the easy part as several of the horses had bells on and the night horse had kept track of them all night long. Then all he had to do was give the horse his head and in a few minutes they would be amongst the other horses. The night horse was very smart about going around the remuda and getting them started in the right direction. Except for the fact that he was Megaliard's favorite roping horse, this was the only work he was required to do and he had done it for many years. He was the key to success or failure. Lloyd just went along for the ride. It seems kind of strange that the horse couldn't be sent out there alone but stick a six-year-old kid on him and he would do it all. The remuda had to be in the corral by daylight so the cowboys could start roping out their mounts for the day's work. If Lloyd was late getting them in he would have to duck a lot of cowboy boots aimed in his direction. Nobody seemed to worry about a kid doing that job.

During the haying season Lloyd was able to help his dad by driving the stacker team. The crew put up the stacks of hay with what in those days was called a "Mormon Derrick." The team would pull on a cable that went through a set of blocks to get the load of hay from the hay slip high enough to clear the stack. The man on the stack would swing it to where he wanted it and pull the rope that opened the slings and let the hay spread out on the stack. Then the stacker cable team would back up to the starting place. The driver of the hay slip would get his slings and lay them on the slip, snap the latch together, and go to the field for another load. The amount of work the stacker team and driver did was directly proportional to the number of slips coming in from the hay field. Before the hay was stacked, it had to be mowed, raked, and put in piles (called "shocks") that were about all a man could lift with a pitchfork.

Putting newly cut hay up in a haystack using a Mormon derrick.

Courtesy of Joe Walters

One day Jim was mowing the hay. The weather had started clouding up and looked threatening. Lloyd was taking a water sack out to Jim and hung it on a cedar tree where it could cool in the breeze. Jim was just starting his third round of the field when a bolt of lightning struck the steel mower and knocked Jim backwards off the seat of the mower. The team got a pretty good jolt also and it spooked them into a run. A working mower sickle, in heavy hay, is hard to pull and the team didn't go very far. They had turned and cut a swath right up through the middle of the field. After awhile, Jim came to and sat up, looking around. He spotted the team out in the middle of the field and the swath they had cut. He hollered at them, "Go ahead and mess it up good. It all has to be mowed anyway." Lloyd knew then that "Old Mancos Jim" wasn't hurt and he rolled on the ground in laughter — not, however, to the enjoyment of Jim himself.

That winter Lloyd went to winter camp with cowboys Tuffy and Arthur Teague. Arthur gave Lloyd a blue-colored mare he had caught from the wild bunch. Lloyd admired Arthur greatly and learned quite a bit from him that winter. Along toward spring they sent Lloyd to the home ranch lying forty miles up the Mancos River. The sky was overcast and looked bad. They said it didn't look all that bad. They were wrong. Lloyd rode as fast as the horse could go over that kind of terrain but about half-way there it started to rain. Then it turned to sleet, driven by a stiff, cold wind. The horse didn't want to face into it and kept trying to turn tail end towards the storm. It was all Lloyd could do to keep him headed in the right direction.

The sleet soon turned to snow and the wind continued to blow fiercely. Lloyd had a saddle slicker with him and put it on. It was old and wrinkled and had been cut off and leaked like a sieve. It wouldn't cover the saddle and Lloyd's legs were wet to the skin. His rawhide boots were soaked and frozen stiff and when he rode into the ranch he was frozen to the saddle. Jim heard the horse and came out to meet them. He lifted Lloyd from the saddle and carried him into the house where Ella helped get him out of the frozen clothes and boots. While Jim went out to put the horse in the barn and see to his care, Ella got a pan of snow and put Lloyd's feet into it and rubbed snow all over them and gradually drew the boy closer to the stove. That was the old-time remedy for frostbite and it probably saved his feet. Next morning Jim took the team and wagon to town to get the supplies that Lloyd was sent after. Four days later the sun came out and Lloyd went back to winter camp with two pack horses of supplies.

These young boys are learning to be cowboys in 1934. The old saying was "start them early."

Courtesy of Joe Walters

They rounded up the cattle from the reservation land in late March. Lloyd left school to help, since he was now the horse wrangler. He was told to have the remuda in the corral by sunup. This time, Lloyd used his own sorrel horse to wrangle on. Like Megaliard's night horse, the sorrel kept track of the horse bells all night long and knew exactly where to find the remuda in the dark. He never failed to find them and get the remuda to the corral on time. During his spare time Lloyd broke his yearling sorrel colt, Sox. The cowboys would be through with breakfast by the time the remuda came in and they would catch their horses for the day and ride out. Then the cook would fix Lloyd a steak cooked on a sizzling hot grill. He never cut a steak less than an inch thick. It would flame up and he would turn it over, right back on the same spot. When it was done he would serve it with biscuits and gravy. The steak was so tender you could cut it with a fork. The cook said the key to tenderness was to age it, to let it hang at least twenty days.

Most of the cattle that were butchered for camp meat were ones that had gotten themselves "rimrocked." This means they had grazed along a bench between two rims and had gone down off some place they couldn't get back up. There was no way to get them out so a cowboy would shoot them and butcher them. Then with some help they would pack the meat into camp. If the weather was a little warm the cook would keep the meat rolled up in a bed tarp during the day and hang it out at night to cool. A round-up crew of fifteen cowboys would eat a beef in about a week. It was served three meals a day, every day.

Cowboys holding a herd of cattle prior to cutting out those beef steers chosen for shipping.

Courtesy of Joe Walters

The crew started the herd up the Mancos River towards the home ranch, when a hard rain developed. Black clouds almost down to ground level made it so dark that you could hardly see ahead of your horse. Lloyd was riding behind the drags (the slowest ones in the rear) when the lightning started popping all around. Since the clouds were so low, the electrical charges in the clouds were all among the cattle. Blue flashes were jumping across cow's horns and occasionally a lightning bolt would travel down a cow's back and jump from her tail across to another cow. The blue sparks were jumping between the horses' ears. Lloyd reached toward his horse's ears and the sparks traveled up his arm — no pain or jolt; just a weird blue light.

The cattle didn't seem to mind the electrical display at all. There are stories of Texas trail herds being stampeded by lightning that frolicked among the cattle. It took several hard days, grazing that herd the forty miles to the ranch but at last they were in the fields and the cowboys were all free to go to their respective ranches. Jim and Lloyd would take care of them until it was time to brand the calves and go to summer pasture. Lloyd went back to school for the next two months and then school was out for summer. He was seven years old.

9: Fights, Jokes and Gambling

Jim and Lloyd went into Mancos one day. Lloyd was sitting outside Uncle George Weber's pool hall, and Jim was in back along the river, building a shed to put their horses in so they would have some shelter when they were in town and Jim was playing poker. Uncle George kept account of the feed bill and Jim would pay him on a somewhat regular basis. Lloyd noticed the town marshal, Jim George, talking with Wesley Dunlap, the sheriff of Montezuma County. Together they started walking down a narrow alley towards where Jim was working. Lloyd didn't know what their business was with Jim. He hadn't been in any trouble that Lloyd knew of. It was nearing dark and Lloyd was waiting for his father to bring the horses out to the street so they could go home.

Jim George came out of the alley first with his hands half raised above his head. He was not carrying a gun. Dunlap came out right behind him and Jim was right behind Dunlap. When they reached the street Jim told them not to look back until they reached the post office. He stood there grinning. He had surprised them in the alley and marched them out to main street with a hammer handle stuck in the back of Sheriff Dunlap. Apparently he had just played a joke on them. He dropped the hammer into the loop in the side of his overalls and went into the pool hall saying, "Lloyd, go fetch the horses."

Marshall Jim George saved Lloyd from getting into some pretty serious trouble in Mancos. Jim had some kind of an altercation with the liquor store owner by the name of Cook. He hit Jim with a pair of "brass knucks" (considered a concealed weapon and lethal) and broke both sides of his jaw. Lloyd was in town the next day on horseback, and went to the cabin where Jim was staying. He was in bed and bleeding from the mouth. With a bandanna Lloyd tied his jaws somewhat the way they should be and got him a drinking straw so he could have water and several varieties of broth. Jim wrote down the name "Cook" and pointed to his jaw.

When Lloyd went to the hitching rail to get his horse, he saw the man Jim had named, standing on the sidewalk talking to someone. Lloyd took down his lariat rope and shook out a loop. He thought that dragging Cook down Main Street would even the score for Jim. Lloyd started his horse into a run to cast his rope when Jim George saw him. He must have very quickly assessed Lloyds intentions because he ran right in the path of his horse, waving his arms and hollering for Lloyd to stop. The horse reared up so high Lloyd nearly slid out of the saddle. Cook saw him at about the same time and ran into the liquor store. The marshal's actions saved Lloyd from committing an act that might have resulted in the death of the man he intended to rope and drag. After Lloyd had time to think about it he was grateful to Jim George. Anyway, before a month had passed, Cook died from pneumonia. Mancos Jim eventually healed up and was back to playing poker.

In Silverton one night Mancos Jim got into a poker game with four fellows, two of which he had never seen before. Lloyd watched the game for a few minutes and then went upstairs to bed. About 3:00 a.m. Lloyd was awakened by his father. He was getting their suitcases together and said, "Son, we are getting out of here, and pronto." They went to the livery and got the team and buckboard. Jim didn't say a word until they had topped Molas Pass. He looked back a couple of times and then began to laugh. He said the two strangers in the game (professional gamblers) were thumbnail marking certain high cards. Jim noticed the markings right away and used them to his advantage. He showed Lloyd $1500.00 that he had won. Jim said he didn't want to fight them so there wasn't any use waiting around until they figured out what happened.

That summer Lloyd was again helping Mancos Jim with the hay. When riding out to irrigate or to go up the ditch, Jim would ride the blue mare, Blue Lucy, that Teague gave to Lloyd that winter down on the reservation. She bucked every time she was saddled up. About the only way that Jim could ride her was to tie the stirrups together with a short piece of rope. By doing this, all a rider had to do was to turn his toes out and that locked his knees under the swells of the saddle and made a much better rider out of anyone. Getting bucked off usually meant a long walk back to the ranch or the cow camp. Since Jim was riding in a pair of irrigating boots he needed all the advantage he could get.

Lloyd had her colt, Sox, to ride and even though he owned Blue Lucy, he never rode her. When Lloyd was breaking her second colt, a buckskin, to lead, the colt set back on the lead rope, and pulled Lloyd's hand around a gate post. Lloyd lost most of the hide from the back of his hand. This really infuriated Mancos Jim and he tied the colt's lead rope to his saddle horn and literally dragged him over on the Mesa Verde side of the Mancos River and tied him to a pinyon tree. He left him to fight the rope until after dinner. Then Jim told Lloyd to go get the colt and lead him down to the creek to water and then bring him to the ranch. Jim had really made a believer out of the colt. All the years Lloyd owned him you couldn't tighten his lead rope. He was that responsive and he never broke a set of bridle reins. Lloyd rode him bareback nearly all of the time and he never bucked with Lloyd on him in his life. He had his mother's endurance, from the wild horse strain and lots of good sense. Thankfully he didn't inherit her ability to buck.

One day Jim and Lloyd went to irrigate. Jim saddled Blue Lucy, mounted her, and she bucked a half a mile out through the alfalfa field. Lloyd was riding along on Sox. Jim said that as soon as he got the water running and properly set for each row they would ride over on Red Mesa and look for strays. When Jim finished with the water, the blue mare wouldn't let him get on with the shovel in his hands. He stuck it in the ground, mounted Lucy, and was riding back towards the shovel to pick it up. When he leaned forward reaching for the shovel, somehow the rope connecting his stirrups went behind the back cinch and Lloyd got to watch another bucking horse contest right down through the muddy hay field. Jim stayed with her until she quit bucking and rode over to where Lloyd was. Both his hands were muddy. He dismounted and washed his hands in the ditch. When he was again mounted he looked over to where the shovel was and said, "That's about where I'll need it tomorrow." They went on over to Red Mesa and tended to the business with the cattle.

That summer Mancos Jim hired two Navajos to help put up the hay. One hundred and thirty acres of alfalfa is too much for one man and a boy. One of the Indians was a small person, lithe and quick. He was a good worker. The other was much too heavy for his size and just a tad lazy. Lloyd had the opportunity to watch them work as he was driving the team pulling the slip that they were supposed to load the shocks of hay onto. The small Indian would load his shock and clean up the leavings. Then he would have to walk around the slip and help the other one load the shocks on that side. Lloyd learned a little Indian tongue that summer. Mancos Jim spoke it well.

About the end of the second cutting of the alfalfa Jim told the small Indian that he could stay and work but he didn't have a job for his partner. The bigger one who was going to be laid off started cussing Jim, and what few words Lloyd knew, he could tell it was rough talk. Jim spoke back in their native tongue and the Indian swung his fist at Jim. It just happened that Jim had a large cold chisel in the side pocket of his overalls. He got a hold of it while fending off the attacking Indian, and laid it up alongside his head. That took the fight out of him real quick. Jim's wife sewed the man's scalp back together with a carpet needle and a horse hair. Jim paid them their wages and they left. Mancos Jim sure had a temper when he was aroused: more ammunition for the growing reputation of a man to be left alone.

10: Skidding Poles

That same fall Frank Stevens bought a bunch of steers in Denver and shipped them on the railroad to Mancos. There were about a 150 head in all. As the Morefield and Pratter ranches on Mesa Verde both belonged to the partnership, they drove them up there and turned them loose. There hadn't been any cattle up there since Morefield proved up on the place and moved out. The feed was good. The steers spent both the winter and summer there without being disturbed. By the next fall they were getting pretty wild. They hadn't seen a cowboy or been gathered in two years. All were branded with a Rafter D so it was pretty likely they would be gathered someplace. Only half of them were gathered on the first roundup. Jim made up a song about them:

Frank Stevens got busy, busy as a bee,
Shipped steers from Denver branded Rafter D
Turned them loose on Mesa Verde below the Morefield well,
Now they see a cowboy coming and run like hell.

Mancos Jim was a good entertainer and played the harmonica and the Jew's Harp. Lots of times after supper, when the cowboys were sitting around the fire, picking their teeth, Jim would play tunes for them. He made up a song about Elliott Magaliard, and on anything that he could get to rhyme. The partnership split up in 1925. Lloyd sure hated to see the end of his cowboy and ranch days.

Mancos Jim got a job at the Gold King Mine in the La Plata Mountains. He and Ella and Lloyd moved into a cabin there at timberline. Jim cut and peeled small timbers for the mine and Lloyd rode the work horse to skid them out. A peeled pole was called a slick. They would dry many times faster with the bark removed. A dry pole was lighter and stronger than a green one. That old brown horse Lloyd used knew more about skidding logs than he did. Lloyd would chain four or five logs together and turn the horse loose down the trail with them. Lloyd would then follow along behind and straighten the horse out if he happened to get fouled up around a stump or a rock. Then Lloyd would ride the horse back to the cutting area. He would always stop and wait at the edge of the clearing for Jim to holler that it was all right for him to come on in. Jim didn't want to have a tree fall on the old horse and Lloyd.

One day Lloyd was skidding a load of freshly peeled poles down the trail and they got to going faster than the horse. The poles still had lots of sap on them and would really slide. The poles slid under the horse between his legs and took his back feet out from under him. This made him sit down on the poles and he rode them all the way down the hill.

Jim got five cents a foot for the timbers he cut and Lloyd got five cents per pole for skidding them out. Lloyd could skid in about three hours all of the logs that Jim could cut and peel in a full day. Sometimes Lloyd would help Jim with the peeling but it was an easy way to get hurt and Jim preferred that Lloyd stay away from the job. This gave the boy quite a bit of free time that he spent in various ways. He saved what Jim paid him for skidding and bought himself a bicycle and learned to ride it at timberline on a switchback trail. He was nine years old and learning to ride that bike at that elevation on such a narrow, rocky trail was a real challenge.

Jack Richner, of Mancos, worked there at the mine also. His job was on the sorting belt as the ore came out of the mine. Lloyd liked Jack a lot and visited with him some when he was waiting for more poles to skid. If Lloyd wasn't spending time at the sorting belt he was roaming the mountains. One day while exploring around he found an old mine tunnel that only went back into the hill about 100 feet or so. It was about four miles from the Gold King. Just inside the portal of that old mine was a stack of several cases of dynamite, about ten in all, and two boxes of dynamite caps and several rolls of fuse. Apparently someone had intended to drive the tunnel farther back into the mountain or do assessment work on claims in that vicinity.

The dynamite and blasting caps had been there a long time and nitroglycerin was seeping out of the wrappers of the sticks of dynamite. That kind of powder is very dangerous to handle and many an innocent person has been badly hurt by it. The standard rule for handling stale powder is to blast it and get rid of it. That old portal should have been closed anyhow before some curious person got caught back in there in a cave-in. Lloyd put a dynamite cap on the end of a roll of fuse and inserted it into the center of the top box. He unrolled the fuse as he went down the mountain towards the cabin. If it burned at about a foot a minute fifty or sixty feet should give him plenty of time to make the four miles home. He cut it off at what he thought was the right length and lit it and took off for home.

This photo of Al Stephens was taken when he was seventy-nine years old.
Courtesy of Grand Junction Daily Sentinel

Lloyd's stepmother, Ella, had grown hard of hearing and didn't hear him come in. He went to his bed and lay down to await the blast. A few minutes later it came and you can bet your Sunday socks Ella heard that blast. It shook the cabin and made the dishes rattle. She asked Lloyd what in the world it could have been. He didn't have an answer for her. The next day after he had skidded the day's cut of poles he was hanging around the belt where Jack was working. Jack asked him if he had heard that big blast yesterday. Lloyd started talking about something else and never did give him an answer. Lloyd thought he was strongly suspected, but he got rid of some mighty dangerous stuff and closed a bad portal.

Mancos Jim and Ella separated that fall. Lloyd never knew what the trouble was. Jim didn't talk about it. Lloyd had grown to like her very much and he knew that he was going to miss that great cooking. Maybe the loneliness was just too much for a woman who had been amongst people all her life. Jim bought a Model T Ford and he and his son headed for Durango. Lloyd can't seem to remember what happened but Jim wrecked the car near Lightner Creek. They flagged down the train and rode it into Hesperus. There they got some help and hauled the Model T out of the creek and got it fixed. The next spring, 1927, Jim and Lloyd drove over to Norwood to visit awhile with Jim's second son, Albert. Al Stephens had just moved down from Telluride where he had been operating a dairy. He leased a ranch in Norwood and brought his dairy herd with him. He planned on milking them, selling the cream and raising hogs, chickens and calves on the separated milk. It worked out fine and he raised a large family while doing it.

Jim and Lloyd then drove over to Montrose and stayed with Jim's oldest son, Walter, who had children older than Lloyd was. Mancos Jim was wanting to get some visiting done, as he hadn't seen any of his family since they had left home. Jim and Lloyd left Montrose after a few days and drove to Portales, New Mexico, where Jim's half-brother William was living. He was a one-eyed man. After a few days in Portales they drove down to Clovis, New Mexico, and Jim got a job on the Agua-Torres ranch. He built fences and as Lloyd had learned to drive the old Model T, he was given a job tending windmills. There were a bunch of them and all had to be greased regularly.

When one of the windmills would quit pumping it was usually a case of the leather cup washers being worn out. Lloyd and some other ranch hands would pull the well pipe out of the ground and replace the worn out leathers. If any joints of pipe were leaking they would be replaced at the same time. These windmills pumped water for the cattle and were a very important part of the whole operation. The Model T traveled the sandy ground pretty well but to travel in the sand washes, which were level as a highway and went for miles, Lloyd would have to let about half of the air from the tires. That gave them the traction they needed.

The work soon ended for them at that place and they went back to Portales and Jim rented a buggy repair shop with a house alongside for them to live in. One evening Jim came home in the Model T and drove into the garage and right on out the back wall. When he got it stopped and saw that Lloyd was watching, he exclaimed, "Who in thunderation is driving this thing anyway?" That fall Lloyd's sister Francis came through Portales, on her way to New Orleans, and Lloyd went there with her to go to school. Lloyd sure missed the times he had with Mancos Jim.

11: *Fighting the Depression*

The great depression of the early thirties had hit and hit hard. A man couldn't buy a job anywhere and if you got lucky and found something, it usually only paid board and room. Lloyd "hobo'd" back to Mancos, riding the rods and the brake beams, to be with Mancos Jim. Tuffy Teague found out that he was home from New Orleans. He came to the ranch one day and said there were still eight head of those Rafter D steers running on Mesa Verde. Tuffy, at that time, owned the Pratter place and was seeing the steers regularly. He wanted Lloyd to help him try to catch them. They were wilder than deer as lots of cowboys had unsuccessfully chased them in their futile efforts to rope one. Tuffy and Lloyd got into the bunch one day and Lloyd roped one. It fought like a demon to get loose and jerked his horse down. Lloyd was actually glad when his rope came loose from the saddle horn and the steer got away with the rope. Tuffy roped one also and it did a forward somersault and broke both horns off. It got away too. They rode back to the ranch empty handed and Jim took care of the tired horses while the two fixed some supper. Jim would have a good laugh at hearing them tell of their wild cow adventure. Those steers must have been nine or ten years old by then.

Late that fall Lloyd trailed one old steer down and ran him off the White Trail into Mancos River Canyon on the reservation. The steer was hot and tired and Lloyd's horse was in a lathering sweat. At that time Bill Gunn was the Chief of the Utes and had a camp at the foot of White Trail and Canyon Trail, which went the other way. When Lloyd got down to where the steer was last seen, old Bill Gunn and his family were butchering him. They were in a pool of water where the steer had waded out and died. Lloyd helped them finish the work of skinning the critter and getting it cut into quarters and packed to their camp. He stayed with them until they cut up some of the meat and fixed a meal. He always boasted that he had a steak from one of those Rafter D steers and enjoyed it in the company of a Ute Chief. Several years later Tuffy sold the Pratter place to the Mesa Verde National Park system and reserved a franchise for the horseback rides to Spruce Tree House.

The early mercantile store built by Bill Exon in Dolores still stands.

Photo by Author

Lloyd started doing some trading around and managed to get some traps that had belonged to Uncle Sol Exon. Cousin Erin Exon gave him a 45-70 rifle that had hung out in the shingle mill for years and years, mainly because Alice wouldn't allow a gun in the house. With it was a full set of reloading dies. Lloyd did work for farmers, traded horses and worked for Uncle Bill Exon in Dolores. Bill Exon raised a lot of potatoes and Lloyd thinks he built the first potato digger. Lloyd trapped and hunted. He once caught a mountain lion in a bobcat trap. His Airedale dog attacked the lion and he had to rush in close, so he would shoot it and not the dog. There was a $50.00 bounty on them at that time and then The Denver Post paid an additional $25.00 for each lion taken. Now a man has to pay for a license just to hunt them. Each puma, as they are sometimes called, needs a mule deer a week for survival. During the depression, the people out in the rural areas depended on the deer for their meat supply. They sure didn't want the lions getting them all.

Lloyd hunted a lot with a cowboy named Scott Teague. He was the father of Tuffy that Lloyd went to the winter range with. Teague had hounds and Lloyd had the Airedale. The reason they work well together is that hounds run by scent and an Airedale runs by sight. The hounds trail game until it is sighted and then the Airedale, who can travel considerably faster, rushes the game and it usually either comes to bay or takes to a tree. This affords easy capture. "Coming to bay" means that the pursued animal, realizing that it can no longer run and get away, finds a corner of some kind, backs into it, and faces the attackers. The money from the bounty and the sale of furs that Lloyd trapped was money that came in mighty handy during depression years. Really, it was all there was. Money was something that hardly anybody had.

For a period of time Scott left the hounds at the ranch and Lloyd took care of them and used them for his own use. One evening during a full moon some coyotes started howling and yipping over across the river from the house. The hounds began howling back at them and caused quite a ruckus. Mancos Jim was getting pretty irritated at the continual chorus of yips and howls and asked Lloyd if he could do something to stop them. The hounds were "Old Rough," a Redbone, and four spotted hounds called "BlueTicks."

Lloyd told his father he would take the Airedale, and when they got out of sight down the river, for Jim to turn the hounds loose. Jim followed the instructions and when the hounds caught up with Lloyd, he turned the Airedale loose with them and went back to the house. There was no more howling or coyote noise but there was quite a bit of dust raised across the river. The dogs all came home about midnight and went to their respective pallets. Lloyd got up and hooked the chains to their collars. The next morning

Jim and Lloyd saddled their horses and rode across the river to where they had seen all the dust being raised. After looking around awhile they found six dead coyotes. They figured the Airedale had killed them working in conjunction with the hounds. They were all very smart and worked really good together. The Airedale would lie in ambush and watch the hounds chasing something. When it came close by where he was he would leap out at it, and in a few seconds, grab it and break its back.

A few days later the Airedale and one of the Blue Tick hounds got loose and before long the men could hear the hound baying on a hot trail. They were on the Mesa Verde side of the river. About the third day, by the intermittent sounds from the dogs, Jim and Lloyd could tell they were back on their side of the river and had worked their way into a side canyon above the ranch. They finally heard the BlueTick baying "treed." Jim said, "Lloyd, go shoot that bobcat and bring the dogs home." Lloyd picked up the old .22 single shot and a half dozen .22 short cartridges. The "shorts" were only fifteen cents for a box of fifty and that was all they could afford to buy.

He found the dogs about four o'clock that afternoon. When he was close enough to the tree to see them and the quarry, lo and behold, he was looking right into the face of one of the biggest old tom cougars that he had ever seen. Here he was with a .22 single shot rifle and loaded with shorts. He could only get off one shot. If he was going to shoot he had better make it a good one. There was some distance between him and the lion. He had to get much closer. He circled back into the trees and crawled on his stomach and hands and knees until he was quite close, dangerously close to a vile-tempered bundle of claws and teeth that had had dogs on his trail for three days. He was nervous and acted about ready to quit the tree and run ahead of the hounds again. Lloyd aimed the rifle for the back of his head and fired. If the shot wasn't effective Lloyd didn't know what he would have done. Maybe God looks after fools and such. To his everlasting relief, with a great crashing of branches, the cat came tumbling out of the tree. The dogs were instantly upon him, for a few minutes getting the only joy they would know for three days of hard trailing.

Lloyd skinned the lion and left the head on the hide. He knew Jim would want to see it. It was a heavy load to carry all that way home. He had the dogs on a leash and was mighty glad to have them with him. There was no moon and it was soon black as only a moonless night can be. That was no problem for the dogs though. They went as straight home as if they had a map and compass. He put the dogs on their pallets and fed them. It was the first meal they had for a while. Jim was in bed when Lloyd got into the house. He threw the cat hide across his body and said, "There's your Bobcat!" Jim reached over to the night stand and got a match and lit the coal oil lamp. He looked the cat hide over and then got out of bed and spread it out on the floor, but with no kind words for Lloyd's efforts or a congratulatory remark. As he climbed back in bed Lloyd heard him say: "Seventy five dollars!"

12: Mules, Sheep and Bear

Jim's friend, Taylor Norton, was out of work and couldn't care for his mules, so Lloyd brought them to the ranch where they could earn their keep. One mule was brown, the other white. The white mule, Old Pete, has his picture in the Montezuma County History Book. For some reason some sheepherders shot Old Pete in the right hip. Lloyd didn't try to dig the bullet out. It was too near the joint and in too deep. It healed up all right but left him stiff in that leg until a certain amount of movement loosened it up. It was in the spring and Lloyd was plowing with Jim's saddle horse and the brown mule. Jim and Lloyd were getting low on groceries: out of sugar, salt, baking powder and most important of all, tobacco for Jim's pipe. Lloyd asked Jim to ride Old Pete the twelve miles into town and get the supplies. Jim's years of being a cowboy formed the basis of his reply: "I wouldn't be caught dead on a mule, much less a crippled one." So Lloyd said, "O.K. you plow, and I will go after the groceries".

Next morning Jim went up to the field to plow and Lloyd saddled Old Pete and started out. It took the mule a while to get the stiffness out but when he did he lit into a running walk. Before the trip was over Lloyd found out he was five-gaited and they were back from town in three or four hours. Jim watched them coming into the ranch. Lloyd rode up to the field and tossed him the sack of groceries. He took out a sack of tobacco, filled his pipe and lit it. During a few puffs on the pipe he studied Old Pete. Pretty quick he said, "Son, get off that mule." Lloyd went to plowing and Jim mounted up and rode the quarter mile or so to the ranch. Next morning he saddled Old Pete and headed for his poker game in town.

When Jim was getting into these poker games, he set a certain amount to lose, and if his luck was bad and he lost it, then he would head for home and wait several days to go back. If his luck was good, sometimes he would come home with quite a bit of money. One night he came home with over $200 and tossed it to his son and said, "Here, go out and buy some stock for this place." Lloyd quickly realized that this was the opportunity for him to try his hand at raising sheep. He bought fifty head of first-year-out ewes. Jim (cowboy attitude again) about had a fit with sheep on the place. He soon got over it and hired a Spanish boy from Mancos and a dog to herd them.

Lloyd bought two yearling bucks from a place several miles away. He carried them home on a pack horse, one in each of the panniers, strapped in. He got a lot of laughs from the people of Mancos as he rode through town on the way home. It probably was a comical sight with those two buck sheep standing up in the panniers, riding backwards, and looking around. The next spring they had a 201 per cent lamb crop. All had twins and a blind ewe had triplets. They had Carl Bell, from Mancos, come down to the ranch and shear them. He said he would shear them for the wool. It brought him forty-five dollars. That fall Jim sold the whole works for over $500.

During the lambing time of the ewes, Scott Teague and Lloyd treed a rogue bear and killed it. When a bear turns stock killer he has automatically put a limit on his remaining days. They are so destructive, especially in a band of sheep. Just a swipe with the front paw, with those long, sharp claws, can rip the udder from a ewe. This is what the bears really go for. The udder is full of rich, warm milk and they love it. The sheep is left to die a long and suffering death. From most any ewe that they kill outright only the udder is eaten. Occasionally a bear will rip open the belly and eat the liver. It is full of warm blood and a delicacy to them. Most stockmen don't wait for a second visit from a ravaging stock killer. They take whatever action is necessary.

Scott got a call from an outlying ranch early one morning. They had over a dozen dead sheep and all signs were indicative of a marauding bear. Scott came to the ranch and got the hounds. The Airedale and Lloyd went with him. Fifteen minutes after they got to where the dead sheep were the hounds hit a hot trail and were instantly on the run. It wasn't a long chase. The bear had gorged himself and couldn't sustain the fast pace of a long hard run. The hounds were soon nipping at his heels and the Airedale was charging him from all directions. He took to the first good tree that would get him away from the dogs. The men were soon at the scene and with one clean shot Mr. Bear was history. They skinned it out, cut it in halves (top half-bottom half), and put a half on each mule to bring it to the ranch.

Jim had brought the two mules for them to pack it in on but he couldn't get Blue Lucy within a hundred yards of that bear. She bucked him off twice and he had trouble catching her so he was way behind the rest of the party. They stopped at the Ed Lewis ranch and he came out to greet them. The moon was shining brightly and Old Pete was carrying the bottom half of the bear. The bear's hind legs were astraddle of the pack saddle, like he was riding it. Old Pete stopped under a weeping willow and there wasn't much visible. Ed hollered out, "Get down Scott and Kid and who is that riding the white mule?" About then Jim and Clarence Hadden came up. They had to tie their horses down the road a ways because the smell of the bear was still too much for Blue Lucy.

A few days after they got home with the bear Jim had some friends drop in for a poker game. They had played a long while and all were hungry. Lloyd had fixed a big kettle of stew and put carrots, potatoes, meat and onions in it and baked a pan of biscuits. They all ate heartily. When the meal was over they all went out on the back porch and sat. One of the guests that Jim called "Rummy Kid" asked him what kind of meat that was that he had eaten. Jim went over to the smoke house where the bear was hanging and opened the door. The upper body half was hanging by a rope around the neck with arms hanging down. When Rummy had taken a good look, Jim said, "Mexican." Rummy immediately lost his dinner. Lloyd thought that was an awfully mean trick for Jim to pull on such an innocent fellow. A skinned out bear hanging upright looks so much like a man that it is frightening to see.

These men are displaying the head of a rogue bear they have killed. The tall man behind the pipe smoker is Sol Exon.
Courtesy of Lorelei Stephens Sutherland

Lloyd left the ranch in 1933 and went to work on Mesa Verde in a coal mine. Jim turned the ranch over to his third oldest son and namesake, Jim, and a woman named Ida Bell who he had with him. Mancos Jim moved into town, got a small cabin and started drawing the old age pension. It was about twenty-eight dollars a month. It was a county payment. Later on the state added to it to make forty-five dollars a month. The depression was easing up some by then and Jim was closer to his poker game. Shortly after that Lloyd went to California and enrolled in a military school. Through his education there he learned the trade of a tin smith and worked at it for several years. Things were looking bad in Europe. Germany was starting to take over all the countries that touched her borders. Someone was going to have to stop them.

In 1939 Lloyd got a letter from Mancos Jim saying that brother Jim had left the ranch and he was going to have to move back there and live on it. Lloyd left California and headed back towards Mancos, Colorado. He made a little side trip down into New Mexico and worked for awhile in a coal mine before coming the last part home. Lloyd found Jim there on the ranch, twelve miles from town, with but one knife, one fork and not a head of livestock on the place. He was down to just a few potatoes, some flour and coffee. Lloyd walked back to Henry Exon's place above Mancos. He was a cousin that Lloyd knew he could count on for help. He loaned Lloyd a horse and saddle and he rode down in the Johnny Pon Draw.

There was a bunch of horses that had been turned out on the reservation by an old man (possibly Johnny Pon) who didn't have feed for them so he let them go to forage for themselves. They were about half wild but Lloyd was able to catch a mare and a stallion. He took them back to Mancos and traded the mare for a saddle, bridle and a catch rope. Henry helped him saddle the stallion, a buckskin. Lloyd mounted him and survived the wholehearted effort he put into dislodging the rider. Lloyd rode back to the reservation and caught three more horses. During the depression time a person could do that kind of thing.

On a trip to town one day Jim and Lloyd rode by the George Geisler place in Mancos where there was a poker game in progress. Jim got into the game with three other men. Lloyd never did care for cards and on the occasions when Jim was playing he would find some place to lie down and rest. He was in another room but was awakened by the sound of loud voices. He got up and went to the room where the game was going on. Mancos Jim was holding a sawed-off shotgun he had wrestled from Geisler. He handed it to Lloyd when he saw him in the doorway. The three men immediately rushed Jim and Geisler. Jim took them one at a time and when there was only one left standing he grabbed his arm, got the nerve hold, and marched him right out the door. The others, when they could, followed. Then Dad turned on Geisler and said, "You don't kill a man any more for cheating at cards." One of the three men had been caught cheating but his pals stayed by him.

Lloyd went to work in one of the several coal mines on Mesa Verde and didn't see much of Mancos Jim. Once in a while they would be at the ranch at the same time. One day when they were there together Jim asked Lloyd if he could fix an old .38 caliber revolver Jim had won in a poker game. The firing pin had broken off and wouldn't fire a cartridge. Lloyd took it over to Ed Zender's blacksmith shop in Mancos, and forge-welded a new piece of steel to the face of the hammer. Then he ground it down to the required size and shape. He shot the pistol ten times, some of it rapid fire, and it never missed a round. Lloyd since wished, a million times or more, that he had never fixed that gun.

13: A Killing

The newspapers hit the streets and the news was like a bombshell to the residents of the normally peaceful town of Mancos, Colorado. The headlines screamed out in the biggest letters they were capable of printing: "NIGHT MARSHAL KILLED." And a subtitle under that: "Frank Lynn Dean shot and killed by James Stephens as the young town marshal was putting him in jail." The newspaper had already tried Mancos Jim and found him guilty. Before Jim was ever arraigned before the Justice of the Peace or any formal charges were filed, the town residents had already formed their opinions, at least the ones who had purchased newspapers. Most of them didn't have to read it. The news spread through the town like wildfire. With every repeated telling, personal opinions were added, until the whole thing was dramatically changed. The only thing that remained constant, and everyone seemed sure of, was that Mancos Jim was the murderer of Deputy Marshal Dean.

It is true that Jim was not well liked in the Mancos area. He had been in too many fights and confrontations to expect to have many friends. Over the years he had earned the reputation of being a bad character. He had lived a hard life among hard people. He asked little and gave nothing. If he wanted to have a few drinks when he felt like it, he did. That was the bad part of Mancos Jim. When he was drinking, he was mean. He was mean enough that very few people cared to cross him. He was raised that way and it was his everyday nature. He didn't go to the liquor store any more for his "booze" since his altercation with the owner and having his lower jaw broken on both sides. He was illegally supplied with his bottle from the bar where he did most of his card playing. The bar, according to law, could only dispense alcohol by the drink over the bar. Jim was their friend and when he wanted whiskey he placed a couple of dollars on a shelf behind the bar down near the end. When Jim was ready to go home he would reach around the corner of the bar and his bottle would be there for him.

The local law enforcement team had to know this was going on. It was too obvious. They overlooked it because nothing serious had come of it so far. On the day of the shooting of the marshal, Jim had been in and out of the bar several times. He didn't stay in there long because there was a young, tough-acting, oil field worker who kept pestering the old man for a drink. It was usually Jim who was soliciting drinks around the bar. Mancos Jim paid him little mind and came and went as he pleased. Still, the guy was beginning to get under his skin a little. Jim at seventy-three years of age could probably have handled the twenty-five year old who had been harassing him all afternoon.

Old Jim had been in hundreds of scraps, mostly with younger people, and he knew all the tricks. Anyone who tried to handle him, for any reason, had better be ever watchful. Lynn Dean, the marshal, knew this and should have been more alert. Jim had been in jail in Mancos a year or so before this episode, accused of hitting an Indian over the head with a club. It may have been self defense. It may have been the Indian he had trouble with at the ranch who came after him to even up the score. When Jim was faced with trouble he didn't give anybody a chance. He looked after himself and did it as quickly and efficiently as he could. Jim went to jail peacefully that time because he was not drinking and knew it would be a short stay.

Mancos Jim at his cabin in 1937. He was age seventy-one.
Courtesy of Lorelei Stephens Sutherland

The night of the killing Mancos Jim decided he would go home. It was about dark. He picked up his bottle from its usual place behind the bar and walked down to his cabin by the river. He fixed some supper and ate. The thoughts of the young fellow who had tried to cause him trouble were still strong on his mind. He had a couple of drinks, then a couple more. His thoughts were on somehow making the tough guy "eat a little crow." Jim wanted to make him feel cheap and insignificant, to humiliate him in front of his friends. That would be good for a young bully with no respect for old age. He reached up on a shelf and got his .38 caliber revolver and headed back to town. The gun was loaded. He kept it that way since a few weeks before when he had to use it to force a couple of freeloaders from his home. They had planned to stay whether he liked it or not.

Jim went back to the bar, entered and sat down at a table near the bar. Later he said his principal reason for taking the gun with him was that he had been wanting to sell it and that very afternoon he had run across a man named Davidson who wanted to look at it. At the trial several people testified they saw him with a gun, and they also swore they heard him say "he might need it." That didn't necessarily mean he planned to kill someone. There were plenty of mean dogs in the town of Mancos, and occasionally a rabid skunk or coyote was seen or encountered in the alleys and back streets. A salesman testified that he saw Mancos Jim hide the gun behind a beverage cooler and then later retrieve it.

While Jim was seated in the bar several people testified they heard him say, "I wish that guy would say something." Other people testified they had heard Jim, during periods of heavy drinking, remark of the times he had killed people because they had crossed him or caused him trouble, or because it was the only way out of a desperate situation. Apparently the tough-acting fellow was leaving Jim alone at that time. Jim got up from his seat near the bar and started to go home again. But somebody had notified the marshal that Mancos Jim was drunk, looking for trouble and packing a gun.

It was the night of October 9, 1939. Lynn Dean had only held the job of deputy marshal for the town of Mancos since Oct. 5, 1939, five days. Perhaps he thought the town should know its money was being well spent and he was on the job and tending to business. By throwing old Mancos Jim into the jailhouse his standing in the town would definitely take an upward course. He may have even thought the old man would be easy. He confronted Jim on his way home. Jim was about a half block from the highway and almost directly across the street from the jail.

Fred McGregor, who had previously served a term as marshal, saw Dean start towards the jail with Jim and he knew from previous experience with Mancos Jim that Dean would probably have more than he could handle. From the witness stand, McGregor said he didn't think Jim was badly intoxicated, because McGregor was following along behind them, to be of some help if necessary, and they were walking too fast for him to keep up. That doesn't sound like a man who should be jailed for drunkenness. Walking drunks home usually takes the whole street and both sidewalks to keep them headed in the right direction.

All Jim might have needed was to be escorted home and left alone. If he was not rip-roaring drunk, Dean could have asked Jim for the gun and told him to go on home and that would have been all there was to it. Small town cops sometimes overlook a lot of things because they have to live there too. That's where they raise their families and everything is much better when the community is running smoothly. The Mancos police overlooked the fact the two partners in the bar were, on a regular basis, filling a pint bottle of whiskey from the bar, and leaving it where Jim would put the money. All the patrons of the bar knew it was going on. Probably the marshal knew it too. But being furnished with this illegal booze, and the mood he was in, probably had a very strong effect on the behavior of Mancos Jim Stephens.

The lightbulb over the door at the jailhouse was burned out that night and it was very dark. Fred McGregor arrived at the jail just a few feet behind Dean and his prisoner. The deputy marshal got the keys from his pocket to unlock the door but had trouble with the lock. McGregor, now just a few feet away, was trying to hold his flashlight on the lock so Dean could see to unlock it. In performing this service for the deputy marshal, his attention surely was directed at the beam of light and he would not have been able to see the moves made by the prisoner. During this unguarded moment Mancos Jim made his move. He struck the marshal from behind and Dean made a grab for him. They struggled, a shot rang out and they both fell to the ground. Dean was shot in the head. The bullet, from where it entered the jaw at about the bottom of the left ear (one newspaper account had it the right ear) veered to the right, passed through the base of the brain and lodged somewhere in the back of the head. Death was instantaneous. The path of the bullet was slightly upward and to the right.

Jim was down on the ground, partly under Dean's body, holding onto the gun, which was resting on Dean's body. McGregor testified that as soon as he saw where the gun was he jumped on Mancos Jim and began beating him over the head with his flashlight and struggling with him over the possession of the pistol. Not once during the trial did anyone ever ask how Mancos Jim was holding the gun, which turned out later to be important. McGregor testified that before he was able to gain possession of the gun he had to whack Jim's hand several times. At this time in his life Fred McGregor had black hair, but before the trial was over his hair turned snow white. He did not live long enough to see the last days of Mancos Jim.

When McGregor was testifying, the prosecutor asked him if Stephens had said anything. He replied, "Yes." The prosecutor asked him to repeat what was said. His statement was that Stephens asked him, "What in the hell are you doing?" The prosecutor did not question him any further about what was said. That statement by Stephens is a very strong indication that he didn't know anything about the shooting of Dean. If he had done the shooting he would have known why McGregor was beating on his head with the flashlight. He would have expected retribution in some form.

Also, if Mancos Jim had shot the marshal, he would have had the gun in his hand in a position to also kill Fred McGregor and be rid of the only witness. After all they don't hang you any higher for two murders than one. If this had been the scene, in the eyes of the law, Jim's case would have been much easier to defend. Without a witness the case would have been very difficult to prosecute. It is very possible that the reason Jim didn't kill McGregor was that he hadn't killed Dean and wasn't concerned about witnesses. The reason that McGregor was able to pounce on Stephens so easily was the dazed condition that Jim was in from the pistol whipping he had received from Dean. Jim's defense attorney completely missed the point on Jim's statement.

Also the possibility of McGregor accidentally shooting Dean in the darkness, instead of Mancos Jim, was finally brought up in court when Stephens had his chance to testify in his own behalf. His version of the case was that he wanted to go home and was on his way home. He met Dean near the post office and the deputy marshal stopped him. Jim said he had a gun and handed it over to Dean. This directly refuted the newspaper account in which they stated that Dean didn't know that Mancos Jim was carrying a gun. It also helped to uphold Stephen's testimony that he was being beaten about the head by a pistol held by Marshal Dean.

Dean said that Jim would have to go to jail and wouldn't let him proceed on his way. He had his arm around Jim's neck and was walking him at a very fast pace towards the jail. When they arrived and Dean was unlocking the door, Jim called him several very foul names and struck him from behind to get loose. Dean retaliated by hitting Jim over the head with Jim's pistol causing a very nasty gash in his scalp. Jim testified that he saw Fred McGregor reach over to take the gun from Dean, there was a shot, and Dean fell to the ground taking Stephens down with him. Dean landed on top of Stephens' legs. Was the gun somehow accidentally fired during the exchange of possession? Jim's testimony was that either McGregor shot Dean or Dean shot himself.

However it happened, McGregor was in a very unique position. If he had killed Stephens he was a hero for upholding the law and coming to the aid of a police officer in dire need. If he killed Dean by mistake he could blame it on a drunken old man, known to be armed, who was resisting arrest and had physically attacked a policeman in the line of duty. He'd still be a hero. Who is to say it wasn't possible? Lloyd tried to persuade Jim's attorney to put him on the stand so he could testify about the hole in his father's thumb web and the bad wounds on his head. The attorney said Lloyd was too young and his brother Al and sister Francis agreed with him.

Lloyd also wanted to bring in another attorney, someone who was from outside the judicial district and wouldn't be "under the thumb" of the district attorney. There was one in Montrose by the name of Charles J. Monyhan who he thought would do a better job for the defense, but his brother and sister both thought he would be too expensive. It was heart breaking for Lloyd that he couldn't be allowed to be of some help to his father, as he was closer to him than any of the other children.

14: Unanswered Questions

❧ At the jailhouse scene Fred McGregor had continued to beat on Jim until he was in a semi-conscious condition and wrested the gun from his hand. All of this had transpired without anyone but McGregor knowing anything about it. There was not another person in sight or hearing. McGregor quickly hid the gun and ran for help. It must be remembered that the sound of the shot was muffled by the bullet first passing through the hem, the pocket, and the collar of Dean's coat. Powder burns on the material attested to this fact. The Columbine Bar and the Exon Pool Hall were the closest places to find someone. A number of people responded and they all went down to the jail.

By this time Jim had recovered from the beating enough to be up and wandering around, staggering towards the highway and home. McGregor went after him to bring him back to the jail but he was so out of breath from running for help that he couldn't hold Jim. The old man, badly dazed as he was, twisted loose, and was finally captured by a man named Frank Kratz whom Jim had bought a drink for less than an hour previous. Jim was still full of fight. He didn't want to go to jail. He didn't feel that they had any reason to jail him and resisted all he could. He later told Lloyd he didn't know what happened to Dean and that he didn't shoot him. He tried so hard to get loose that finally Frank Kratz leveled him with a very hard punch to the jaw and with other help they threw Mancos Jim into a cell. For the second time in five minutes Jim was reduced to a semi-conscious condition.

Lloyd went to see his father in jail the next morning after the shooting. He had been terribly beaten about the head with wounds that no flashlight could possibly have made. The doctor came while Lloyd was there and administered to the lacerations and remarked that they were very bad. Jim's defense lawyer did say that he thought all flashlights were too flimsily built and would never hold together long enough, while being used as a club, to cause that kind of wounds. That is about the extent of the remarks that Lloyd remembers hearing in Jim's defense. At least a week passed after the shooting episode before Jim began to regain his mental capabilities. After all, he had been pistol whipped by Dean, beaten with a flashlight by McGregor and slugged in the jaw by Frank Kratz, all in a period of five minutes or so and while the seventy-three-year old man was intoxicated. Lloyd never thought that Fred McGregor told all there was to tell because he only answered the questions that were put to him. Plenty of things went unanswered.

Jim's request for a change of venue contained nineteen well established reasons why Jim Stephens could not get a fair trial in Montezuma County. Listed among the exhibits was the claim that threats of mob violence were known to have been circulated among the people of Mancos, particularly in the Mormon Church of which Lynn Dean was a member and whose father was a bishop. Stephens lost the change of venue when the prosecution produced fifty witnesses who swore in an affidavit that a fair and unprejudiced trial could be held in Montezuma County. Could it be possible that some of the same people who on the night of Dean's death were ready to take mob action and just a few days later swore in an affidavit that a fair trial could be held? Were they even a part of the jury pool?

Probably the only reason that the mob violence thing didn't materialize into a reality was the town-imposed ban on public gatherings due to an infantile paralysis scare that was circulating the area at that time. Even the funeral service for the slain deputy was held at the cemetery. Friends had paid their respects at his home where the body lay in state. The cemetery gathering was very large.

The defense attorney had no plans to go up against an eyewitness murder case. His only plans were to try and get a change of venue and to get a mistrial. Early in the trial he was advised by Rose Stephens, wife of Albert Stephens who was the second son of Mancos Jim, that she had seen the wife of one of the jurors (whom she knew personally) pass a note to her husband as the jury was filing out at the end of the day's proceedings. When the change of venue was lost, Jim's attorney asked the judge for a mistrial, on the grounds that the jury had been tampered with. The investigation of the incident did not show any tampering. The envelope handed to the juror contained his toothbrush and a five dollar bill.

After Jim lost the change of venue the incomplete testimony of McGregor was never brought up again. Also the claim of prejudice by the entire town and county against the defendant was wiped out by the prosecution's long string of witnesses. One of the very men, from whom Jim had taken a shotgun just a few years previous, to keep him from killing a card cheat and his two partners, sat on the coroner's jury and pronounced Jim guilty of murder in the first degree.

Fred McGregor couldn't read the fine print on the barrel of the alleged murder weapon when he was asked to identify the make of the gun. He could, only after great difficulty and some coaching from the deputy district attorney, make out the caliber of the cartridges. He had first identified the gun as a .32 caliber but changed his testimony after it was pointed out to him, again by the deputy district attorney, that one of the cartridges was a .38. He couldn't identify the gun by sight, because he had not seen it clearly the night before, but said he knew how it felt in his hand when trying to get it away from Stephens. The deputy district attorney had him identify it by the feel of it. Do you think he could have possibly picked it out, by the feel of it, from four or five pistols all similar? Lloyd thought that was the most ridiculous admission of evidence that he had ever heard of. He didn't think there was any way it could have happened as explained by the prosecution witnesses.

Fred McGregor was carrying a flashlight for no other reason than to help himself get around town after dark. Lloyd was inclined to believe McGregor's eyesight was poor, at best, and probably very bad at night. In fact, if he tried to intervene in the scuffle between Dean and Stephens, dark as it was, he could not have known one combatant from the other. If he tried to use a gun at that time he could have very easily shot the marshal by mistake. More proof of his poor night vision was the fact that no one was able to find Dean's keys. If Dean was shot the way McGregor said he was, the keys would have been hanging in the lock or would have dropped straight from his hand to the ground. Trying to reconstruct the scene at the jail, that fateful night, requires a lot of speculation.

The whole case against Mancos Jim Stephens seemed to be mostly speculation. Every one assumed that he shot Dean, because McGregor said he did, and they didn't look any further for evidence. Fred was their eyewitness. Lloyd believes that Jim was just as good an eyewitness that Fred reached around behind Jim and took the gun from Dean's hand and then there was a shot. Shouldn't one man's word be as good as another's? Apparently not, when one of them is an old man, known to like his bottle and who had been in lots of trouble, and the other an ex-marshal with the sentiment of the town behind him.

There was just too much about this case that was never explored during the course of the trial. From the position where McGregor stood, holding the flashlight for Dean to see to unlock the jail door, it would seem unlikely that he could see Mancos Jim pull out a gun, and shoot Lynn Dean from behind. It would be doubly doubtful if McGregor had the vision problems that he appeared to have at the coroner's inquest. The bullet was never removed from Dean's head and through the science of ballistics matched to the alleged murder weapon. Jim Stephens' fingerprints were never proved to be on the alleged murder weapon. Dean had handled it. McGregor had handled it. He gave it to a man named Joe Piccone who handled it and he gave it to the coroner, J. W. Ertel, who handled it.

Jim didn't have any legal counsel at the coroner's jury. He could have used some. The coroner's jury was supposed to establish the cause of death, and if they knew for sure, they could write in on their ballot who they thought was responsible and if it was felonious. To have to go to trial with a guilty verdict from the coroner's jury was very bad publicity for Jim. It certainly didn't reduce the public sentiment against him. If the verdict had been "by person or persons unknown," as it should have been, the prejudice felt by the community might not have been so high.

All things considered, Fred McGregor had the same chance to kill Dean as Jim did but he was never questioned as to any part that he may have played in that night's tragedy. Jim's family believes that a properly conducted trial would have brought out much, much more and possibly it was what Fred McGregor was hiding that caused his hair to turn white during the course of the trial. They believe the district attorney didn't go after McGregor because Mancos Jim was a man they could convict with very little expense to the county and one whom the townspeople of Mancos would like to be rid of.

15: *Lloyd's Story*

While Lloyd was visiting his father at the jail he noticed a bloody spot on his hand. It was a puncture through the web of skin between his thumb and forefinger. Jim didn't remember anything about how he got it. It could have been caused by a whack from the flashlight. When Jim's pistol was introduced as evidence it was noted that there was an empty chamber among the five cartridges that were in the cylinder. That was normal as all careful people who carry a revolver have the firing pin resting over an empty chamber. That prevented an accidental discharge of the weapon in case it is dropped or subjected to a hard blow. If Jim had drawn the pistol from his waistband, or coat pocket, and shot Dean as Fred McGregor said he did, the bullet would probably have gone straight through Lynn Deans' head from back to front and he would have dropped like a rock.

McGregor never mentioned a struggle of any kind but the two bodies went to the ground locked together with Dean's body on top. That seems to indicate there was a struggle and that the testimony of McGregor may have deviated from his original report. The testimony stated that Dean was attacked from behind and shot from that position. If that was the case the first cartridge to the left of the empty chamber would have been the one that fired. Inspection of the pistol showed that the first bullet to the left of the empty chamber had been passed over and the second one was fired. The first one was not a misfire. There was not a mark on the cap (primer) which would undoubtedly have been there in the case of a misfire. The whole episode suddenly became clear to Lloyd. He believes Jim when he said he didn't kill Dean. Lynn Dean shot himself and here is the only way Lloyd could figure that it happened.

Lloyd believed that Jim was relieved of the pistol before they started the walk to the jailhouse. The marshal had been called and warned that Jim had been drinking, acting disorderly and was carrying a gun. Fred McGregor had heard Jim say that he was an old man, maybe a little drunk, and he would go home when ever it damn well suited him. Taking the gun away at that time would be in keeping with good police practice. It is utterly absurd to think that a police officer, or anyone trained to fill that capacity, would ever try to take an ornery drunk to jail while he was armed and considered dangerous. To search and disarm him would be the first move for the policeman to make.

When Jim saw his chance he struck the marshal at the door of the jail, not to kill him but to get loose. Dean retaliated by beating on Jim with the pistol, hence the scalp wounds too severe to have been administered by a flashlight. To prevent further beating Jim grabbed at the gun. In the darkness he couldn't see how he was holding it. Neither could Fred McGregor upon whose testimony the entire case was based. The web of skin between his thumb and forefinger was under the hammer of the gun and Dean tried to shoot it. The needle-sharp point of the firing pin perforated Jim's skin, which prevented the pistol from firing. Dean pulled the trigger again. This time Jim may have lost his grip a little. The conflict had to be intense. His hold on the gun may have shifted towards the barrel where he would have enough leverage to direct it away from himself, not necessarily towards Dean but away from his own body. The web of skin was no longer in the way and when the trigger was pulled all the way, the cylinder rotated to a new cartridge, and the gun fired. Hence the second bullet, instead of the first, was fired. How else could you explain it?

Dean and Jim were locked together in a life or death struggle for possession of the gun. Somehow as they were falling Dean's body was in such a position that the bullet passed through the hem of his coat, the coat pocket and the collar of the coat before it entered his head in a slightly upward course, veering to the right in its path through the base of the brain. That would prove the body was in motion, probably falling, when the bullet entered the man's head.

Jim gained a ninety-day stay-of-execution when he filed, through his attorney, an appeal to the Colorado Supreme Court at the expense of Montezuma County. The court declined to enter the order but stated they would allow District Attorney Noland and defense attorney McKelvey to appear before the Supreme Court and argue the merits of the appeal. The outcome was that Jim's attorney would be allowed to file an abbreviated and informal brief. In essence this meant that the Colorado Supreme Court never saw a word of testimony. Montezuma County was spared the expense of a transcript, usually a heavy expense item. The Colorado Supreme Court examined the case to see if all correct procedures had been followed. When it was clear to them that all judicial procedures were correct they disallowed the appeal. By a vote of five to two they confirmed that Mancos Jim should die on June 21, 1941.

Whether all of this is the way it happened or not doesn't really matter now. Lloyd has merely wanted to have a chance to tell his father's side of the story for a long time. It has bothered him considerably that a man, who he believes is innocent of murder, may have been sentenced to die for an accidental death. He recognized that Mancos Jim Stephens was hated and feared by most of the residents of the town. He believed the local newspapers already had him tried, convicted and sentenced. The district attorney must have kept at the jury with the theme of motive, opportunity, Stephens being the owner of the alleged murder weapon, and his place at the scene of the crime.

Mancos Jim was mean and given over to periods of drinking. Lynn Dean was the town favorite — the cream of the crop. Members of the Dean family had been in Mancos almost since its beginning. They had been church and business people and well respected. Lynn was born and raised in Mancos. He was a star athlete and played on a championship Mancos basketball team that went all the way to the state tournament. He had married the prettiest girl in the pep club and they had a daughter three years old. It's a terrible shame that he was taken from his wife and baby at that time.

But bad as Jim was, Lloyd believes that he didn't deserve to die for something not entirely his fault. It cost the ranch and everything that went with it to pay the costs of the trial, and Lloyd never thought they were fairly represented. Lloyd believes there was ample evidence, had it been brought to the attention of the court, to have caused the jury to have reasonable doubt. That is all that would have been required to remove the death sentence that was hanging over Jim. It might even have meant acquittal.

Lloyd believes that Jim should have had the change of venue that was denied him on the most meager of grounds. He feels that Mancos Jim would never have been convicted of first degree murder in a town a hundred miles away. Jim was sort of the town drunk and drawing an old age pension. These pensions were a huge drain on the county funds. A long, drawn-out trial, with a possible change of venue, would have been devastating to the county's treasury which had been severely depleted by incomplete and in some cases, non-existent payments of taxes. The country was just beginning to recover from the throes of the great depression. Vindication for the death of Lynn Dean would be the life of Mancos Jim.

16: 7 Hoss

After the trial was over Lloyd didn't feel very welcome in Montezuma County. His family had lost everything so there was nothing holding him to that area. He went to work for North Continent Mines' Inc. as a millwright. The selective service draft of October 1940 called him for military service. He went into the army along with Jess Robinson who had been sheriff of Montezuma County after W.W. Dunlap was killed in 1935. He served over four years in the European theater of operations and took part in five major campaigns. His knowledge of the Navajo and Ute languages was a small help to the officers who had to translate from "code talkers" to the English language. Code talkers were a vital link in sending battle information back and forth from headquarters to the front lines. The intelligence officers didn't have to take time to code the messages. It was spoken in the native dialect of the Utes and Navajos. The code was never broken.

In 1942 (left to right) Chester Hawkes, Tommy McMann, unidentified man, Jack Greager, Tom Stephens, Vernon Ladd and Jess Robinson, former Sheriff of Montezuma County.
Greager Family Collection

After the big war was over, North Continent Mines, Inc. didn't have a job for Lloyd, so he went down to Uravan, Colorado, and hired on with United States Vanadium Corporation. They were later to become Union Carbide and still later Umetco, Inc. He went to work there as carpenter foreman and retired from that position. When signing work orders and such he used the abbreviation for Thomas, "Thos." But he had a habit of not fully crossing his "T's" so what he wrote looked like "7hos." His friend Jerry Moore started calling him 7hoss and a considerable number of people still call him that today. In fact, Jerry made up a poem about him and the name 7hoss.

Ode To 7Hoss

Look over yonder upon that hill,
See that man sitting his horse quiet and still.
That's the cowboy known here 'bouts as 7hoss,
And everyone around shies clear, 'cause he's the boss.

He can ride any bronc no matter how mean,
And he's the best man at rop'n you've ever seen.
No man can beat him in a rough and tumble fight,
And Lord help you if he's look'n at you, over his rifle sight.

He's rode this country from one end to the other,
And the Ute Brave always calls him Brother.
But now 'ole 7hoss's trail begins to grow dim,
And he sits his rocker with his memories around him.

By Jerry Moore

Lloyd wrote the following poem in 1943 while he was overseas in the Army.

Trappers Time

Just before daylight,
In the early hours of morning,
I start on my days occupation,
A job that is cold and forlorn.
I hunt the fur bearing animals;
I'm an expert with a horse and a gun.

I ride the hills by daylight ;
I never get home by dark ,
And care for my pelts by lamplight.
The fur is silken and prime.
A trapper has a weary time,
A life that is dull like mine.

My trapping will be ruined in a century
By people moving west by time;
My hunting will be stopped by fences.
Herds of cattle and sheep in the pines
The animals too few to be taken;
The pelts will not be prime.

When I'm old and weary,
I'll be content to sit and pine,
To think of the days of adventure
Winter months and trapping the line,
Riding, hunting and fishing,
Caring nothing about old age or time.

Reaping the fur from the animal,
Sowing the traps on the line.
And at the turn of the century,
Cattle, sheep and their kind.
I'll think of the days gone forever
And the fun that I've had in my time.

17: Jim's Execution

Even condemned to death Jim outlived eleven of the twelve jurors who convicted him. He was sentenced to die in the lethal gas chamber at Canon City, Colorado, on June 20, 1941. Sentence was carried out in the presence of Warden Roy Best and thirteen witnesses who included a chaplain, a physician, a surgeon and a sheriff. When Jim was seated in the chair he showed no emotion. Stoic indifference had been his attitude ever since he was placed on the witness stand and his testimony and plea of "not guilty," seemingly ignored, and he was more or less given a polite legal rebuff. The attendants came with the black hood to cover his head.

No one expected any kind of trouble from the old man as he was in such a weakened condition from several weeks in the prison hospital that he had to be carried from his cell to the gas chamber. A lot of his confinement time had been spent in the prison hospital. A bout with pneumonia was just about his last but he finally recovered and built up enough strength to have all of his teeth pulled. His diet was mostly fruit juices, eggs and other soft foods.

Just as they placed the hood over him, from the depths of his lungs, he let go with a screaming Comanche death cry and pulled his left arm free of the restraining strap. It chilled the blood of every person in the room. He had struck terror to their hearts. With one sweep of his arm he jerked the black hood from his head. Total silence reigned. Perhaps they could feel a little of the emotion that he was keeping hidden so deep inside. They were all speechless and immobile. It was some time before the crowd regained their composure. The attendants again came forward apprehensive that another death cry might be forthcoming. With trembling hands the black cloth was again placed over his head. The arm and leg straps were tightly secured. "Cinch them down good, boys, you don't take any chances with Mancos Jim," he said.

All was ready. The warden pulled the lever and the cyanide pill dropped into the sulfuric acid. Deadly hydrocyanic gas enveloped the prisoner. In exactly nine minutes James Stephens, number 21450, was officially pronounced dead. He was the oldest man ever to be executed in the State of Colorado or the entire United States — age seventy-four years, six months, fourteen days. Warden Roy Best stated to the assembled crowd that they had just witnessed the toughest execution he had ever had to perform. Mancos Jim is buried in Lakeside Cemetery near Canon City. A requiem mass was held at St. Michael's church by Father Schaller. Mancos Jim had accepted the Catholic faith while on death row.

Lloyd got a letter from Mancos Jim while he was overseas in the Army. It was written just a few days before his death. He wrote these heartbreaking words: "Well, it's about time, Lloyd. The old man with the scythe is just beyond the door. I didn't kill Dean. You know I would never shoot a boy."

"It matters not I have oft been told,
Where the body lies when the heart grows old."

BOOK TWO:
The McDaniels Brothers and the Westfall/Dunlap Murders

1: *An Old Cowboy is Murdered*

James Westfall was a cowboy from the early days of the West. He had lived through the Indian troubles of several different areas and loved to tell about the stirring days of the cattle and sheep wars in Wyoming and his experiences while working there. He was given over to rough talk about the early times and often adopted a threatening attitude when deeply involved in telling some long-ago saga of outlaws, vigilantes and such. All who knew him discounted this behavioral pattern because they knew him to be generous and hospitable to the extreme. As he lived alone in his home about a mile west of Lewis, Colorado, and a short distance off the main road, he was eager to have people stop by and visit. The latch string on the door was always on the outside.

Sometime during late April or the first few days of May 1935, James Westfall had visitors. What they left behind was a scene of savage and carnal waste. Helplessly bound and gagged, seventy-seven-year-old James Westfall was left to die alone in his home by a fiendish person or persons. People in the vicinity began to notice that neither the old man or his dog had been seen for about a week, so on May 5, a Lewis couple, Mr. and Mrs. John Alligier, went to investigate. James Westfall had befriended them when they first moved to the country and their anxiety was aroused when the first reports began to circulate of the dog being locked in the house for several days. The Alligiers had to look through a couple of windows before they could make out the old man's shoes sticking out from behind the bed. Mrs. Alligier then entered the house and found the body. Noting the bindings on both hands and feet, she was certain of foul play and they left to summon officers.

Coroner E. E. Johnson and Deputy Coroner J. W. Ertel were summoned to the scene immediately after the gruesome find. After a careful preliminary examination of the body, they ordered that it be transported to the morgue in Cortez. District Attorney

James R. Noland was called over from Durango and a coroner's inquest was held Monday afternoon May 6. Officers investigating the murder were quite perplexed by the absence of clues to the guilty person or persons.

Examination of the body before the coroner's jury disclosed that Westfall's hands had been securely tied behind his back with a strip of bright plaid cloth and an old rag. His knees had been bound with an old rope and his ankles tied together with another rag and a towel. A gag fashioned from a piece of dirty cloth was rather loosely tied over his mouth. This had slipped part way from his face and was covered with froth. The froth had congealed in a manner that indicated breathing after he was bound. More evidence indicated that he had struggled to free himself for hours as ante mortem bruises were found on the hands, wrists, knees and ankles where the bonds had been fastened, and the back of the head had been bruised and cut. This last wound caused momentary belief that he had been clubbed but since there was no fracture of the skull it was decided that the bruises could have been caused by the victim striking his head on the floor as he struggled to free himself. A bruise in the middle of the back was also probably caused by the same fall.

The final verdict of the jury, composed of E. S. Porter, C. R. Neal, James Filey, C. R. Hickman, G. O. Harrison and T. P. Kuhre, was that Westfall had come to his death at the hands of a person or persons unknown, and that death was due to exposure and exhaustion in an attempt to free himself from the bonds fastened upon him by said person or persons. The inquest also served to attach robbery as the motive for the crime.

J. T. Westfall, a nephew, testified that he saw his uncle alive the last time on April 13. At that time Westfall showed him no money but he said it was customary for the old man to show his money freely. The nephew knew a sum of fifty dollars had been sent to the victim a month or so before by a sister, so he believed it probable that he had money at the time of his death. None had been found on the body or about the house. A Colt automatic pistol, a double barreled shotgun and an axe were also missing. Mrs. Alligier also testified to the habit of Westfall to take in strangers for the night and show his money freely. County Assessor J. G. Dunning was thought to be the last person to see Westfall alive when he testified that he had seen him crossing the road near his home. At the time of the inquest it was reported that Rev. Paul Shields saw Westfall alive on Sunday, April 28, just a week before the body was found. The consensus on the case was that Westfall was murdered by someone whom he had probably befriended by providing shelter during the bad weather the last of April. He was robbed of his money, probably a trifling sum, and left helpless to die in the cold house.

District Attorney Noland took the lead in the investigation and worked on several leads furnished by people living in the area. One very promising bit of information led the officers to the community of Red Mesa, Colorado, where they encountered Herbert McDaniels and began questioning him about some very peculiar behavior the community residents had noticed. What seemed strange to them was that Herbert, who had been married only a few days, about the time it was reported that James Westfall was found dead became very edgy, remorseful, and had taken to drinking heavily. His bride seemed terribly unhappy. The officers questioned him about his activities over the previous two weeks. He immediately broke down and confessed to the murder of James Westfall and implicated his older brother, Otis, age thirty.

District Attorney Noland had the cooperation of the *Montezuma Valley Journal* in withholding this information so that apprehension of the older man would be more likely to follow, but upon his return to Durango the evening of May 10 from a trip to New Mexico, he called the newspaper to release the story. Indications were that Otis McDaniels would be arrested even before his brother was arraigned before Justice of the Peace L. E. Tripp.

Herbert McDaniels, who was the man actually held in jail, confessed that he and his brother came to Westfall's home on April 28 for the express purpose of robbing him. The old man had been spotted as a likely victim by the older brother, who stopped by Westfall's a day or two before. After binding him and taking twenty dollars cash, the two guns and the axe, they left him helpless. Young McDaniels told authorities that they believed the victim would live to be released. They then made their way southward and that night stole an automobile belonging to Professor Offil at the Arriola schoolhouse. In it they returned to Red Mesa where they had been living.

In the succeeding days they dismantled the car, burning the body and tossing the engine into an old well. These were some of the strange actions that had been reported to authorities Sheriff W.W. Dunlap and District Attorney Noland. The destruction of the car would have left the case without a clue but for some chance remarks that reached the ears of an alert schoolmistress who sent the officers on the right trail. The older brother, Otis, had already left the Red Mesa community before the officers closed in on Herbert. Otis had a bad reputation throughout northern New Mexico and Arizona. He had also seen prison time in Utah. In 1928 he was convicted of grand larceny in McKinley County, New Mexico and was sentenced to ten to fifteen years in the penitentiary. He served three years and was released on good behavior.

Early Friday morning, May 17, Otis McDaniels surrendered himself to the sheriff of La Plata County at the home of his father-in-law, Arthur Zufelt, of Red Mesa. District Attorney Noland reported that McDaniels had returned to that part of the country with the intention of giving himself up to try to save the life of his younger brother who was charged with the murder of James Westfall. The older Otis stated that he was the leader in the robbery of the old man. His confession tallied closely with what his brother, Herbert, had already told officers. Otis McDaniels was brought to Cortez and arraigned before Justice of the Peace L. E. Tripp, at five o'clock Friday afternoon. He waived a preliminary hearing and was immediately returned to Durango to await trial in district court in July.

After the capture of the pair of murderers the entire three-county area, Dolores, Montezuma and La Plata, was so incensed over the brutal slaying of James Westfall that talk of lynching the pair was heard from every corner of the area. In fact, angry crowds had assembled and threatened to forcibly remove the pair from the jail and take them to a spot and hang them. Sheriff Wesley W. Dunlap was very concerned for the safety of his prisoners and fearing that the Durango jail was not a secure place for them, he immediately ordered them removed to a place far out of the area where they were being held. The new escape-proof jail in Glenwood Springs, Colorado, was where the pair was sent and they remained there until it was time to bring them back to the July session of the district court. District Attorney Noland and Sheriff Dunlap had agreed that they would go for the death penalty for both of the McDaniels brothers and that was the way that Noland proceeded to build his case against them.

2: A Gallant Peace Officer Goes Down

The pair of murderers had to be returned to Durango, so during the week prior to July 15, Sheriff Wesley W. Dunlap was looking around in Cortez for a deputy to make the trip with him to help out with the driving. J. L. (Lem) Duncan was not doing anything at the time so Dunlap made him a deputy and they made the trip to Glenwood Springs to return the pair for trial. They left with them Sunday morning, shackled and handcuffed in the sheriff's car and started on their way to Durango. They stayed all night in a hotel in Grand Junction and the next morning early they drove to Montrose and fed the prisoners breakfast. After a rest stop the party started on their way once more. When they reached the town of Placerville there was a decision to be made as to the route to follow to return them to Cortez — whether to return by way of Rico and Dolores or by way of Norwood and Dove Creek.

For whatever reason Sheriff Dunlap apparently chose the latter route and they were proceeding down the San Miguel River canyon on Highway 145. This highway was a dirt and gravel road at that time with only a few wide places to turn out when meeting a car. Chances are that there wasn't more than a half-dozen cars at most traveling this route on a given day so it wasn't likely that very many would be encountered. One car, driven by Norwood resident Clyde Vaught, had the misfortune of running off the road about nine miles west of Placerville the day before and the driver was slightly hurt, leaving some blood stains in the seat of the car.

When the car carrying the Dunlap party reached this point, the Sheriff asked the driver, Deputy Lem Duncan, to stop as he wanted to check out the car and see if anyone was still in it, possibly hurt. This was done and Duncan remarked to the sheriff that he had been thinking of stopping anyway as he suspected that there was a tire going flat. Back in those days, flat tires and over-heated radiators were the two most common road problems that a motorist had to put up with. Most everyone carried jacks, tire patching material, tire pumps and extra water in canvas water bags, as they were always cooler to drink out of.

Several times on this morning's trip, the McDaniels brothers had complained of their shackles and handcuffs being too tight and because of the July heat and sweat the officers had stopped and relieved the pressure of them somewhat. During the morning's trip, Sheriff Dunlap had placed his revolver in a pocket that was on the inside of the front door, within instant reach from his seat, should trouble develop. Dunlap had been warned by other law enforcement officers that they didn't think Otis McDaniels had given himself up solely to save his younger brother from the murder charge that was now hanging over him also. Their thoughts on the subject were that Otis wanted to be with Herbert so that he could engineer an escape if ever the chance presented itself. Otis had seen penitentiary time and been with hardened criminals and would be a serious threat to deal with in an escape attempt.

Sheriff Dunlap got out of the car but did not take his revolver with him. That moment of carelessness cost him his life. As he walked back up the road towards where the car was off to the side, Lem Duncan leaned out from the driver's seat to inspect the tires on that side of the car. At the instant that Duncan was leaning far out from the seat of the car, the McDaniels brothers, in perfect unison since they were shackled together, reared up over the back seat of the car. Herbert shoved Duncan the rest of the way out of the car and Otis grabbed the sheriff's gun from the door pocket. They ordered the deputy to stay face down in the dirt of the road and they scrambled out of the car.

After Sheriff Dunlap had completed his inspection of the wrecked car, he climbed back up to the road and started walking back toward his own car. It was then that he noticed that all wasn't right with his deputy and the prisoners. While Herbert stood with his shackled foot on the deputy's neck, Otis turned the gun towards Sheriff Dunlap. The sheriff, being a fearless man and knowing that he had to persuade Otis to give up the gun, walked calmly towards him, talking to him about all the trouble he was in and advising him not to make it worse by anymore bloodshed and noting they were in such a remote area that escape would be almost an impossibility. He continued walking towards them, still talking about their giving up the pistol and when almost up to Otis he held out his hand and asked him to hand over the gun. The reply was a blast from the revolver and a bullet that went through the sheriff's hand and into his right shoulder, knocking him to the ground with the deputy. In this helpless position Otis stepped around behind him and from a slightly stooped position placed the muzzle of the gun behind the right ear of the sheriff and pulled the trigger. Sheriff Wesley W. Dunlap's life was over. Just a careless moment and it was the end of everything.

Otis then got Deputy Lem Duncan to his feet and told him if he wanted to live to take off up the road as fast as he could run and not look back. This he did and he ran until a turn in the road hid the car from his view. The McDaniels brothers then retrieved the keys from the body of the sheriff and unlocked the shackles and handcuffs from their wrists and threw them into the brush. Then they got into the car and sped off down the road at a reckless rate of speed as though they had to leave the ghost of the dead sheriff behind.

They had only driven a short way but had reached a considerable speed when they met a woman driving towards them. She was a Mrs. Cuthbert from Naturita, Colorado. She later testified that they were going so fast they were only hitting the high spots in the road. After she met the sheriff's car, driven by the escaped prisoners, she soon came upon the supposedly dead sheriff lying in the road. She stopped and tried to get the body into her car but was unable to do so and continued on towards Placerville.

The Civilian Conservation Corps (CCC) Camp in 1936 near Norwood where Dr. Goldberg was the resident doctor.
Greager Family Collection

Just a short way up the road she saw Deputy Lem Duncan who was trying to get off the road and into the brush. He thought her car was the escaped prisoners returning. She hailed him and he came to the car and got in with her and told of the episode that had just happened. She told of meeting the speeding car headed downriver. As soon as they reached Placerville they called the sheriff at Telluride and reported what had happened. They also stated that the supposedly dead sheriff was still alive and to bring a doctor. The doctor from the Civilian Conservation Camp (CCC) in Norwood, Dr. George Goldberg, was also summoned by a group of men from this same camp who had gathered at the site in Placerville where the body was lying in the road and had tried to give him comfort. They stayed there until other help arrived.

The next car to come up the river road towards the sheriff's car was one driven by Glenn Ruffe of Placerville who had a daily mail route from there to Paradox Valley and return. The escaped prisoners had already driven the sheriff's car off the road and quite a way down into the oak brush that bordered the river. Ruffe had seen the top of the car from up on Norwood Hill where he had a good view of the area while traversing the last half mile of the hill. After he crossed the bridge and proceeded up the road, he said the car was not visible from that side of the river. When he arrived at the scene of the shooting, the body of the injured sheriff had already been removed to the hotel in Placerville to await the arrival of the doctors and the sheriff.

Another photograph of the CCC Camp near Norwood showing the individual squad quarters.

Greager Family Collection

San Miguel County Sheriff, Guy Warrick and a doctor from Telluride arrived at Placerville at just about the same time as doctor George Goldberg from the Norwood CCC Camp. Together they did what they could for the victim and transported him to the hospital in Telluride where he died about four o'clock that afternoon. Sheriff Warrick immediately called Montrose County Sheriff A. M. McAnally, Ouray County Sheriff Jess Woods, Game Warden Lem Ballard, and Brand Inspector Sam Phillips and they in turn notified their deputies and any officers who were familiar with the country that was going to have to be searched for the escaped criminals. That evening they all converged on the tiny community of Placerville to be briefed on the happenings and to plan the search. Governor Edwin C. Johnson was also called and told of the brutal murder of Sheriff Dunlap and he immediately called the National Guard for an airplane to be sent to the area with an observer, to fly over the terrain and aid the searchers in any way possible.

3: July 16— Day One

By noon, some 300 men were combing the hills in every possible area where escaped criminals could have chosen to hide out. The airplane was circling low over the terrain and had agreed to drop white flags to indicate the location of the hunted men should they sight them. That morning while Glenn Ruffe, the mail carrier to Paradox Valley, was traveling down the San Miguel River Road and was nearing the bridge at the foot of Norwood Hill, he encountered Sheriff Warrick and a large group of men with whom he stopped to talk. He advised them of the location of the car top which he had seen the day before from higher up on Norwood Hill. The sheriff and his men had seen no trace of the quarry and were trying to decide what to do, as there was another road which continued on down the river and eventually climbed out of the canyon on a road built by the Norwood Camp of CCC boys. It eventually would take a person to Montrose via Sanborn Park, Horsefly, the Dave Wood Road and Springcreek Mesa, a route the bandits might have chosen to travel. Glenn Ruffe said that he did not stop that morning to investigate the car as he was unarmed and feared the hunted men might still be in that vicinity.

Sheriff Warrick and his men surrounded the car with sawed off shotguns and revolvers in hand ready for action but the car was abandoned. Normally, the San Miguel River is very difficult to cross by a person on foot. Mid-July would still be a rather high water-time. The San Miguel is considered one of the fastest rivers in Colorado over its entire length. But on this date in 1935, things weren't quite normal. The area had been in the throes of a drought during which 1934 was the driest year ever seen by the people living there. Perhaps the flow of the river was not so wild and swift as with normal runoff. They took up the trail of the killers which led down to the river and it was noted where they slid down a bank to the water's edge.

One of the men of the posse said he would test the river's force to determine if the McDaniels brothers might have been able to cross. He almost lost his life in the attempt. That the pair of fugitives might have crossed the river now seemed out of the question and the sheriff decided they should look somewhere else for the fugitives.

Several of the searchers went down to the bridge and crossed to the other side where it was determined that the criminals had, in fact, crossed the river. They were tracked part way up the hillside before all sign was lost. At this point, Sheriff Warrick pulled the men off the trail and went to Placerville and called the penitentiary at Canon City to send a bloodhound or more than one if they could spare them. They responded by sending three: one, known as "Chief" to be worked alone and a pair named "Beau" and "Bess," in charge of their keeper, Charles Angell of Canon City.

Since Norwood was the closest town to where the known trail of the outlaws began, the bloodhound Chief was left there. This author's father, Dewey Greager, owned a pool hall in Norwood and in the back part was an ice house with lots of sawdust which would make a good bed for the dog. My dad agreed he would keep the dog and since he had three grown sons, all in their early twenties and eager to join the search, they might work out to be a team. I can remember, as a child of eleven years, on certain days, going back to the ice house and putting out feed and water for the bloodhound. We were warned to stay clear of him and not to "rattle his chain."

The airplane landed on a hilltop strip near Norwood to take on fuel and to report any sightings of the fugitives. There was nothing to report. The pilot, Lieutenant Houghton, and observer Sergeant Burnell said the Norwood strip was too small for the new Curtis Observation plane and they would not land there again. Montrose would be their base of operations from then on.

4: July 17 — Day Two

Most of the sheriffs working on this manhunt figured that the fugitives would try to make it to the area of their homeland at Red Mesa, which is not many miles from the border of New Mexico, and if they could escape into there, help would be everywhere for them. They had many friends among the Indians on the reservation as it had been reported that Otis McDaniels was a frequent whiskey peddler on the back roads and trails where the trade could be carried on with little chance of being caught. The only trail that had been found so far was where the fugitives had crossed the river and were on the south side. If they continued going south, they were headed for New Mexico. This is where the day-two search was concentrated.

All the land was searched from the San Miguel River south as far as Dunton and east towards Wilson Mesa. Chief and two of my brothers and about a dozen other heavily-armed men set out for a point where it was thought the killers would top out from climbing the canyon side. In a surprisingly short amount of time the bloodhound picked up a scent and started on the trail. But something was wrong, terribly wrong. The trail was going down the canyon side. How could this be possible? It should have come up the hillside and continued any direction but down. But that was the only way the dog would go. Perplexed, the men sat down and tried to figure out what the fugitives had done. Had they gotten a look at Lone Cone Mountain, a landmark for several hundred miles around and decided that New Mexico was well over a hundred miles away, cross country, and they had better try using another route to get there?

This seemed to be the general thought among the posse so they let the dog take the trail again and it led them back down to the river's edge. All the men in the group were afraid to cross the river afoot. They said it was too swift and they might perish. The McDaniels brothers had crossed it, not once but twice, but they were desperate men and fleeing for their lives. The posse went down river to the bridge at the foot of Norwood Hill and crossed to the north side and went back to where they had left the scent across the river. The dog picked up the trail again and worked his way up to the road. Here he became confused. Lots of traffic had been on the road because of the excitement of the manhunt and the scent had been scattered and obliterated in places. Sometimes the dog would turn and go down the road a ways but would give that up and try to pick up the trail again upriver. This was about the end of any usefulness that was obtained from the bloodhounds.

Since no one had seen any sign of the wanted men, lots of wondering was going on in the minds of the men in charge of the groups in the hills doing the hunting. Had a passing motorist, not knowing who the fugitives were, given them a ride out of the country? They certainly seemed to have disappeared into thin air.

5: July 18 — Day Three

A report came into Sheriff Warrick of San Miguel County that the two desperados had been seen in the vicinity of Dunton, Colorado, on the west fork of the Dolores River. This renewed the original thinking that they were trying to get to the Red Mesa area and possibly from there into New Mexico. As quickly as it could be arranged, the team of bloodhounds, Beau and Bess, and their handlers, were transported to the Dunton area and began searching the area for the trail of the fugitives. In their report to Sheriff Warrick the searchers said they picked up the trail but followed it only a short ways when they came upon a band of sheep that had crossed in front of them. They reported that the dogs were unable to find the trail again. Acting upon a pure hunch, the search party went down the road leading towards Rico and then decided that Priest Gulch would be a good place to search. The dogs could not find any kind of scent in that area either and then it started to rain, so the search was called off for that day.

While this search was in progress, James Noland, the District Attorney from Durango took a crew of twenty-five armed men and went to the La Plata Mountains to search there and to try to head off the wanted men if they had succeeded in crossing the Dolores River in the Priest Gulch or West Dolores region. Nothing was found in that area, but over one hundred men were left patrolling the road down the Dolores River and several roads and trails leading into Red Mesa.

" Shoot to kill" were the orders issued by Jess Robinson, the newly appointed sheriff of Montezuma County. A description of the wanted men was flashed to all parts of southwestern Colorado. Otis McDaniels was described as five feet three or four inches in height, about thirty years of age, weight about one hundred and fifty pounds, brown hair, gray eyes and ruddy complexion. Herbert McDaniel's appearance was similar except that he was thin, weighing possibly one hundred and thirty pounds and he was nineteen years of age.

At this time, a group of men under Deputy Joe Hess of Nucla took the searchers down the San Miguel River road below the bridge at the bottom of Norwood Hill and thence up the newly constructed road following the old Indian Trail that leads to Sanborn Park and the Horsefly region. The posse searched for any sign all across this area and when they reached the divide road on top of the Uncompahgre Plateau, they turned west toward the town of Nucla where they ended the search for that day. A report had reached the deputy that a pair of men matching the description of the wanted men had been seen crossing a Forest Service road in a heavily timbered area. The fugitives were believed to be armed with at least one revolver and a knife but their ammunition might be limited to not more that four rounds. The search conducted by Joe Hess and his party netted absolutely nothing. Sheriff McAnally from Montrose returned to that city on the evening of July 18 and said he would await further developments before joining the search parties again.

6: July 19 — Day Four

Word reached Sheriff Jess Robinson of Montezuma County that at approximately 4:30 p.m. of day four, two young men answering the description of the McDaniels brothers appeared at the home of Maggie Menafee and her mother, three or four miles from Mancos, Colorado on a direct route from the place where the murder of Sheriff Dunlap took place toward the Red Mesa area. They jumped over a fence and came up to the front gate of the Menafee home near Menafee Switch. The younger one acted as if he wanted to go to the house but was held back by the elder one and they continued their way down the railroad track. A short distance away at the Glenn Robbins place they shot a sheep but before they could possess it, Robbins came out. The men then left in a hurry. Both families reported to the sheriff that they were positive in their identification of the two men.

The pair of bloodhounds was still in the area and District Attorney James Noland was able to get them to the area of the sightings by 11:00 p.m. and they were placed on the trail. Many reports were being circulated at this stage of the search that the posse was hot on the trail of the McDaniels brothers and their capture was imminent, possibly before morning. How wrong they were. Who they were trailing was never known and on that very afternoon of the reported sightings, the McDaniels brothers were robbing a sheep camp on Hastings Mesa not twenty miles from the scene of the killing of Dunlap. They had come through the small community of Placerville in the night of day one and stolen two pairs of shoes from the back porch of a residence. One pair was a woman's overshoes and the other was a pair of shoes that Herbert was able to wear while Otis wore the overshoes.

That afternoon, a young man named Raymond Pritchard, who was working on Hastings Mesa for Lee Arizuma, a local sheepman, came to Montrose and reported to Sheriff McAnally some suspicious actions of a couple of strangers who had contacted him Friday. Pritchard was a very reliable young man and said he hadn't heard of the murder and subsequent escape of the criminals but he sensed something not quite right about them. They had a ragged appearance and one of them was wearing women's overshoes in the hot July weather. After he fed them a meal that consisted of two pounds of cheese, three cans of baked beans and a whole Dutch oven of cold bread and other things in proportion, they asked if there was another camp in the area.

Pritchard said he took them to the camp of Frank Williams, a Mexican. The two men talked with him for a while but did not stay at this time. Otis conversed with the Mexican in his native tongue which he would have been very capable of as he had spent much time among the Mexican people of northern New Mexico. The two men left the camp of Williams, and Pritchard returned to his own camp. Later that afternoon he walked down towards the highway to an old cabin that he knew of in the area. The men that he had previously fed had told him their car had stalled down on the highway. He looked around for automobile tracks but found none. He then looked in the cabin and the two men were in there and hurriedly jumped behind a partition as though scared but did not pull a gun.

That evening the fugitives came to his camp and again asked for food which was given them. The men then left his camp and when they were out of sight, Pritchard made his way down to the highway which crosses Dallas Divide, caught a ride into Montrose, and by telephone, reported to Sheriff McAnally what he had seen. Apparently he believed that his camp was not in San Miguel County, hence he did not call Sheriff Guy Warrick.

In the meantime, the wanted men had made their way to the other sheep camp and again ate everything the herder had cooked and then loaded up a sack of canned goods and disappeared into the thick timber. The criminals had been just a day ahead of the searchers and were never anywhere except the San Miguel River Canyon and a short trip to the top of the canyon side when they crossed the river and climbed out. They immediately went back down to the river and crossed again and with extreme care proceeded up the road towards Placerville, hiding in the heavy brush whenever a car came along.

7: July 20 — Day Five

More men were enlisted for the search for the killers of Sheriff Dunlap. In the Mancos region the men were certain that they had the fugitives surrounded and in just a few hours their capture was assured. Not one speck of vigilance had been relaxed in any part of southwestern Colorado. All available men from Cortez, Rico, Dolores, Mancos, Telluride and from all parts of Montezuma, Dolores, San Miguel, La Plata and Montrose counties joined in one of the biggest man hunts ever staged in western Colorado.

While a posse back-tracked over the faint trail lost the day before in the rain-soaked mountains east of Cortez, funeral services were held by the Elks Lodge of Durango for W. W. Dunlap of Cortez. Almost everyone from the entire area not connected with the search for his murderers was present at the funeral. Flowers were banked high against the wall of the chapel. Even while the funeral services were being conducted, eight picked men who knew every inch of the country to be searched took the bloodhounds and went into the mountains to try once again to straighten out the trail of the two men who had been reported in that area and identified as the wanted men. The Red Mesa area was still being closely watched as the prime suspect area that the murderers would try to get to.

At the same time, a report reached the sheriff's office from Silver City, New Mexico, sent by Owen C. Matthews, Sheriff of Grant County, that he was leading a hastily formed posse to the Willow Creek region in the Mogollon mountains ninety miles to the west upon receipt of a report that a ranchman had found a car (a Ford v-8) said to have been abandoned by Herbert and Otis McDaniels, the slayers of Sheriff Dunlap. Sheriff Matthews said the car carried Colorado license plates and that it answered the description of the machine driven by two men identified in Socorro, New Mexico late the previous night as the McDaniels brothers.

The two men had also reportedly been seen passing through the town of Mogollon earlier that morning. Tally B. Cook, the sheriff of Socorro County, reported to Matthews that the men were recognized at Socorro by a filling station attendant. Sheriff Matthews said credence was added to the belief that the two men were the wanted men because the McDaniels at one time lived on a ranch near Buckhorn, sixty miles west of Silver City and they had relatives in that area. All available officers and men were pressed into service in the hunt, the sheriff said, and he had all roads and trails into the Willow Creek section blocked off.

Even though the killers of Sheriff Dunlap had been seen, fed and positively identified and their location assured on day five, reports continued to come in from various sections of the four-state region.

8: July 21 and 22 — Days Six and Seven

Reports from Shiprock, New Mexico, only fifty miles south of Cortez, stated that the McDaniels brothers were being sought in that region. Continued and conflicting reports from the Navajo Indians in the section rear Red Rock, fifty miles south of Shiprock, brought a posse of San Juan County officers from Aztec, New Mexico, into that section, seeking the wanted men. R. J. Vaughn, senior clerk at the Navajo Agency at Shiprock, said Indian police reported the Aztec officers had returned home after their investigation failed to disclose any worthwhile clues.

Meanwhile, northeast of Gallup, New Mexico, officers were investigating various rumors locating the slayers in that section. A posse composed of Chief of Police Presley Kelsey, Undersheriff R. R. Rogers and Deputy Sheriff Bob Roberts, all of Gallup, left early after receiving reports the brothers were seen the day before on the western slope of Mount Taylor, northwest of Grants. At the sheriff's office in Gallup it was reported also that Jess Robinson, the newly appointed sheriff of Montezuma County and deputies Frank Weaver and Jim Henry investigated

BOOK TWO: The McDaniels Brothers and the Westfall/Dunlap Murders ◉ 87

and found without basis, another report that the fugitives were hiding in a cave fifteen miles southwest of Grants. Explaining the reports which came out of the reservation for that week concerning the McDaniels brothers, Vaughn said the Navajo Indians had been in a state of excitement since tracks of two men were found south of Gallup. The Indians claimed the tracks were made by two white men.

Back in Colorado the search was being concentrated on the eastern end of Hastings Mesa, the top area of Dallas Divide, the Horsefly region, the area leading down into Pleasant Valley, and the area southwest of Ridgway, Colorado. Reports persisted in Ridgway that the outlaws were about to be surrounded and brought in. Someone had telephoned to the town marshal of Ridgway that the two men had been seen in the West Dallas Creek area and this report was probably true. It was probably only the second true report that had come in so far. Men were dispatched to search this area but the hunt was without success.

Then a report was sent in during the noon hour that the two men had been captured in Happy Hollow, close to Ridgway. This report was soon found to be untrue. At this time all the manpower that had been searching the areas around Mancos and Cortez and along the Dolores River from Rico to Dolores with their team of bloodhounds responded to the call to come to Ridgway and join in the search as the men had been definitely seen and identified close to that town. The old bloodhound Chief that was being cared for by my father in the sawdust pile behind his pool hall in Norwood, had been called back to Canon City as he was needed there. My two oldest brothers still continued to help in the manhunt. I can remember quite vividly their returning home late in the evening — tired, wet and discouraged from days of finding nothing. They always leaned their rifles up in the corner behind the front door so they would be handy for a quick grab if they were called out hurriedly.

Nearly all of the rancher families living on Hastings Mesa and the surrounding areas moved their women and children into town as they felt that the ranch outposts would be the first places the fugitives would go looking for food and shelter. Also the cowboys and other people living in the high country during the summer months felt they would be able to keep a better eye out for the criminals and have more freedom in trying for the $250.00 reward, dead or alive, that had been placed on the head of each of the McDaniels brothers.

Help for the fugitives by way of automobile was considered a possibility and two suspicious cars were checked out. The first was a car that later proved to be loaded with canned goods, a bedroll and plenty of gasoline that made several trips up and down the San Miguel River at about day three as though they were looking for someone. The car was later stopped near Whitewater, Colorado, and inspected by police before it was allowed to go on. The second instance was on the afternoon of day eight when word was sent to have officers watch the roads for a black sedan with a Denver license that had passed through Ridgway under suspicious circumstances, with two men in the back seat evidently holding a gun on the driver. The car was not seen by any of the men alerted to watch for it.

There was so much excitement and so many wild rumors it was impossible to keep track of events. However, the facts are that nothing more was seen or heard of the wanted men in that area since Otis McDaniels had conversed with Frank Williams, the sheepherder. The outlaws had made it to U. S. Highway 50 about two miles north of Ridgway and from all appearances had caught a ride from someone, going in an unknown direction. As was later found out, they had caught a ride into Montrose where they walked the full length of Townsend Avenue about five o'clock on the morning of day ten. Out on the north end of town they later caught a ride which brought them back through Montrose and took them quite a few miles on the road toward Gunnison.

While the manhunt was being so actively pursued in the neighborhood of Ridgway, a reporter from the *Montrose Daily Press*, John M. Addington, decided to spend a day with one of the posses that were combing the hills south of Baldy Mountain and in the vicinity of the Crawford sawmill which was situated well up into the black timber of Dallas Creek. The press felt it would be a fine time to have a reporter on the scene as it had been reported that the killers were bottled up and capture was likely to take place at any time. Being in a crowd of people during an exciting event is also a great time to sell subscriptions.

Almost everyone had at least one gun showing. One little man weighing about one hundred and twenty pounds and wearing a deputy sheriff's oversized badge, had a big six-shooter strapped to his hip and was carrying a long-range rifle in the crook of his arm. The keeper of the bloodhounds had a big automatic strapped to his leg and was wearing a pair of binoculars around his neck. It looked like the old West being re-enacted or election day in the Ozark mountains. After a hard morning's work and nothing to report, Mr. Addington returned to Ridgway and while mingling with the crowd, did sell one subscription to the "best little daily in the U.S.A." — the motto of *The Montrose Daily Press*.

9: *July 23 and 24 — Days Eight and Nine*

One would think that robbers would pick Ridgway as the very last place in which to stage a robbery during the time of the greatest manhunt in Colorado's history. Everyone in town was sleeping with one eye open and a gun nearby. However, to add to the excitement the town had been experiencing, burglars actually picked Ridgway to stage a robbery on July 23. Perhaps the robbers reasoned that all the dangerous and best marksmen were out in the hills and the town would be wide open for a heist but such was not the case. About 1:30 a.m., as two men were busily engaged in removing the contents of the Boucher Drug Store on Main Street, their actions became so noisy that they awakened a Mr. Harvey, across the street from the store that was being looted in wholesale fashion. Seeing the sidewalk in front of the store littered and cluttered up with goods, including a cash register, a slot machine, and many other boxes of goods, he decided something should be done.

Mr. Harvey was not a resident of Ridgway. He was an advance

man for a comedian show which would be coming to Ridgway in the following week. Having been awakened by the noise of the drug store's front door being broken down, he grabbed up a rifle and went down to the scene of the robbery and fired a shot. The robbers reacted very quickly, one plunging out a rear window to escape in the car they had placed in the alley, but the other came out with his hands up and Mr. Harvey held him until help came.

Sheriff Jess Wood of Ouray was summoned and took the prisoner back there for investigation. The prisoner would not talk. The one who got away had a flour sack filled with candy, cigarettes, cigars, wrist watches and other goods but in his sudden and desperate flight he left the stuff behind. So far as is known he got away with nothing but his life. It had been noted that a car with a Grand Junction license plate had been seen in town that afternoon and evening and it was suspected as having been used by the robber in making his getaway. Sheriff Wood notified officers of surrounding towns. It was about 2:00 a.m. when Wood called Sheriff McAnally who hurriedly got out but just as he got downtown, an attendant at a service station said a car with a Grand Junction license had gone down the road with the throttle wide open.

There was nothing new in the search for Otis and Herbert McDaniels. The latest search had been concentrated under the shadow of massive snow-capped Mount Sneffles when a large posse combed the hills in an effort to flush out the desperados. A week had gone by since Otis McDaniels talked with the sheepherder, Frank Williams, on Hastings Mesa. Whether the brothers were still in the Hastings Mesa region or whether they had drifted out of the country, was not known. Many thought the two slayers obtained a ride out of the country while some thought they were still holed up in the region above Ridgway. There were many avenues by which they could have gotten clear out of the country undetected. They had a food supply and with renewed strength and purpose they might have been able to get over the country faster than was previously thought. When they reached the top of Dallas Divide they would have been provided with a good view of the country and would know the proper route to travel as they had recently traveled over that part of it in the company of Sheriff Dunlap and Deputy Lem Duncan.

Meanwhile, reports were still coming in from northern New Mexico in the vicinity of Thoreau and Ambrosia Lake of the body of a man found dead in an abandoned automobile and the New Mexico authorities connected the McDaniels brothers with the slaying. Local officers discounted the report as false but they could not be positive.

10: July 25 and 26 — Days Ten and Eleven

More information on the alleged killers of Sheriff Dunlap surfaced when the sheepherder for Burl Herman reported to his employer that he saw two suspicious looking men at 2:30 Sunday afternoon, July 21, come from his camp. They quickly disappeared in the timber when they saw they had been noticed. The herder stated that they had cleaned out his camp of all cooked foodstuffs as well as a lot of canned goods. This particular sheep camp was in the Horsefly region which is basically across the Dallas Divide highway to the north of Hastings Mesa and perhaps five or six miles away from the camp of Frank Williams.

Two days later some people traveling the Forest Service road on Iron Springs Mesa, which lies several miles to the southwest of Horsefly Mesa, reported seeing two men cross the road and disappear on the northwest side, which would be in the general direction of Nucla. A description of the two men was not given but searchers went to the area anyway as all reported sightings had to be checked out whether they had any basis in fact or not.

Surmising that the fleeing killers had seen the country from the top of Dallas Divide and knew what lay that direction and then proceeded over to the Horsefly region and then went to Iron Springs Mesa and from there got a good look at what lay in that direction, which is basically where they had started from after the murder of Sheriff Dunlap, it is logical that they preferred the view offered from the top of Dallas Divide and the inviting possibilities of U.S. Highway 550 traveling north and south just below them. As it later proved out, this is the route they chose.

11: July 27 — Day Twelve

¶ The ride that was afforded the McDaniels brothers on the early morning of day ten apparently didn't carry them any farther than Cimarron and when they had alighted from the car they must have heard a train whistle in the Black Canyon and headed that way as hopping a freight would be a much safer way of traveling than on the highway that had so many unprotected stretches where they would be exposed. The train crew from the east upon arrival the afternoon of July 27 reported to the officers seeing two suspicious looking men in Black Canyon near Curecanti, who had taken to the brush as soon as the train crew saw them. It was believed they might be the McDaniels brothers so the Gunnison County sheriff was notified to keep watch at the end of the canyon.

12: July 28 — Day Thirteen

¶ In today's world of crime and corruption you hear so many people say that the laws are made to protect the criminals and too many times they are permitted to go free or receive a sentence far too light for the enormity of the crime. Read what the Editor of *The Montrose Daily Press* had to say on that subject on July 28 while the search for the McDaniels brothers was being carried on:

> The ease with which the McDaniels brothers who murdered Sheriff Dunlap of Cortez a couple of weeks ago, have escaped the united clutches of the law thus far, if they are still alive, shows that the criminal has all the best of it when he is out in the open in a rugged and moun-

tainous country like that in which they are supposed to have made their rendezvous since their escapade. And when the officers do meet up with them—if they are brought in alive—and they get into court, they will have all the best of it with the vast protection the law throws about them to escape the punishment they so richly deserve—the gas chamber.

All the peace officers in this part of the state, bloodhounds and airplanes have concentrated from Ridgway to Mancos following every possible clue to overtake them. They are alleged to have been seen at cattle camps, which they ransacked for food. Suspicious characters have also been seen lurking in the forest fastness, reports to the sheriffs disclose. Several hundred men have spent days and nights in the mountains looking for them. Thousands of citizens have been on the *Qui vive* hoping too get a glimpse of them. Relatives of the murderers had a car running around in a suspicious manner doubtless attempting to make contact with them.

If alive they may get out of the country, since they have escaped capture so long. The officers, however, will pick them up before long, no matter how far they get away. They will be back at the old game of crime they have been following for years. They are jail and penitentiary birds, but the leniency of the law permits them to soon get out after they have engaged in criminal acts through our rotten parole laws—and then they go at it again. How tremendously our law-enforcing officers are handicapped in the detection of criminals and how discouraging it must be for them to try to get law enforcement when they are balked at every move.

In the case of the McDaniels brothers, while I have not been on the manhunt and know very little about it, I have always been inclined to the theory that they were drowned in the San Miguel river when they attempted to cross it since the water was so high and so swift and they were possibly hand and leg cuffed together. I hope they did meet their fate in this way and that Montezuma and San Miguel counties may be spared the expenses of a trial. AMEN !

13: July 31 and August 1 — Days Sixteen and Seventeen

¶ An exceedingly good break came in the case of the McDaniels brothers when Uri Hotchkiss called *The Montrose Daily Press* and said that at the meeting of the Taylor Grazing Act Advisory Board at Delta on Wednesday, Owen O'Fallon, a rancher just east of Gunnison, told the board that he believed he entertained the McDaniels brothers at his house the previous week. He said that two men, very tired and worn out, appeared at his house one day that week and asked if they could rest for a few hours. He told them to go to the bunkhouse. They said they had walked all the way from California and were worn out. This would be believable as 1935 was still considered part of the great depression and there were hundreds of men riding the boxcars and hitch-hiking along the highways looking for a little work to earn a meal and a little rest.

When the two men got ready to leave they started out through the field and O'Fallon called to them and told them that they could not get out that way. They replied that they wanted to walk on the grass or soft ground, as their feet were very sore and one had on a pair of women's overshoes.

O'Fallon then asked his young son to see if he could find a pair of old shoes he could give to the one wearing the overshoes. The boy found a pair and the fellow put them on. They then went on their way. Later O'Fallon got a picture of the McDaniels brothers from Sheriff Lockhart of Delta and identified them positively as the two men who had stopped and rested at his place. O'Fallon said he had read about the crimes they had committed but he had not kept up with the case and had not suspected the men. The *Montrose Daily Press* was by far the most active in the pursuit of information and was now offering a $500 reward.

14: August 2 and 3 — Days Eighteen and Nineteen

Otis and Herbert McDaniels must have had a lot of good luck catching rides in spite of their bedraggled appearances, with heavy mustaches, long beards and long and straggly hair. They were only one day getting from a ranch just east of Gunnison until they showed up on a ranch near Salida where they worked about a day and a half before they resumed their flight ahead of the law. Their route now was down the Arkansas River but signs showing that they were nearing the state prison must have prompted them to take off on a highway leading to the South Park region.

They soon reached the little ranching community of Guffey and there they applied for work in a hayfield at the Orin Carey ranch in lower South Park. As it happened, another Guffey rancher, Gene Rowe, who had been hunting some of his cattle on Black Mountain, rode into the Orin Carey ranch just as the two McDaniels brothers were asking for a few days' work. The timing was right for the two men as this was the time of year when there was much work being done in the hayfields. They were told that work was available and they were put up in the quarters for hired men.

15: August 4 and 5 — Days Twenty and Twenty-One

Gene Rowe, a cattleman accustomed to noticing things, had taken a good look at the two men applying for work at the Orin Carey ranch. No thought of the McDaniels brothers had entered his mind until he was riding along towards his home. Upon arriving at his ranch he looked up an old newspaper that had the wanted men's pictures in it but he wasn't completely sure that those were the two men in the hayfield. He gave it a lot of thought over Sunday, August 4, and Monday morning he drove down to Canon City and talked to Bruce Andrews, the undersheriff. Andrews had a more recent picture of the men and gave it to Rowe, who drove back to his ranch feeling pretty certain that he had the murderers of Sheriff Dunlap identified and located.

16: August 6 — Day Twenty-Two

On Tuesday morning, Gene Rowe had some cattle that he needed to have a look at in the Black Mountain country so he rode his horse through the hayfield where the two men were working. He stopped to chat a while and a glance at the photos was the clincher to their identity. Rowe rode back to his ranch and called Bruce Andrews. In about an hour Andrews was at the Rowe ranch with some prison guards and then they all drove in cars over to the Carey ranch. The group met Sheriff Neal Brown of Park County on the way over. He and Andrews led the men into the hayfield. Gene Rowe stayed in the car as there were plenty of men for the job.

The hayfield near Guffy, Colorado where the McDaniel brothers were captured.

Photo by Author

The officers spread out around the two men, one of them was on a hayrack and the other on the ground. The sheriff yelled at them and when they saw the guns they put up their hands but denied being the McDaniels brothers. They gave their names as Paul Hamblin and Bob Williams of Delta, Utah. They didn't have any guns on them and were easily handcuffed. The older one tried to act awfully gruff and mean and the other trembled a lot but they went along without trouble. Despite their protests, officers brought the two men to the penitentiary for further questioning and finger printing. As soon as fingerprints were made and compared, the two men broke down and confessed they were the McDaniels brothers.

At long last the grueling search had ended. The murderers were behind bars and were being questioned about the two murders they had committed. Most of the early questioning was about the "starvation murder" of James Westfall, as District Attorney James Noland wanted to get the case ready for fall term of court in Durango. He planned to ask for the death penalty for both of the McDaniels brothers. He could probably get whatever he asked for in his district. Feelings had run so high that lynching of the killers was a distinct possibility, and they had to be moved out of the area to prevent that from happening. That was what got Sheriff Wesley W. Dunlap killed, moving them back for trial.

District Attorney Haywood of Grand Junction thought the murder of a policeman should take precedence over the killing of a non-law-enforcement person. He wanted to try the McDaniels brothers in Telluride first and if he couldn't get the death penalty for them, then they could be turned over to James Noland for prosecution for the murder of James Westfall. Noland felt sure he could get the death penalty and stubbornly refused to give his consent for the pair to be tried first in Telluride. Finally, however, he consented to have the pair tried first in San Miguel County. The pair of murderers was brought from Canon City prison to the jail in Grand Junction on Thursday under heavy guard including western slope sheriffs and two district attorneys. The prisoners were kept in Grand Junction until their trials were set in Telluride, the county seat of San Miguel County.

17: The Questioning

It was claimed that the brothers, in their confessions, made some statements regarding Deputy Sheriff Lem Duncan, involving him in some manner in their escape. There seemed to be enough credence to their story for Sheriff Jess Robinson of Cortez to pick up Duncan and transport him to Rico where he was turned over to Sheriff Guy Warrick of Telluride. He was then taken to the jail in Telluride where he was held for questioning.

It seems that neither of the McDaniels brothers told the same story and both of them differed somewhat from the story first told to Guy Warrick by Lem Duncan. Assistant District Attorney Charles Fairlamb grilled Duncan thoroughly all morning Friday about the killing of Sheriff Dunlap. District Attorney Haywood and Police Chief Decker of Grand Junction took over at noon after coming into possession of the story told by the McDaniels brothers. They hoped to iron out the discrepancies in the stories being told.

Otis McDaniels claimed he and Duncan were long-time friends, that they had made whiskey together during prohibition and sold it to the Indians on the reservation. He also claimed that he had once worked for Duncan herding sheep up on the headwaters of the Dolores River. Otis claimed that he and Duncan had gone to dances together and were even friendly with the same girl at one time. Otis also claimed that Duncan had bought some candy for him and his brother on the trip down from Glenwood Springs, and at one time had intimated that he wished there was some way that he could help them. Otis further stated that when Lem Duncan put the shackles around their legs, they were so loose, all they had to do to get loose was take off their shoes and they slipped right off. Otis also claimed that Duncan was wearing a holster with a revolver in it and that was the gun that was put in the pocket of the front car door, supposedly for the convenience of the prisoners, according to McDaniels.

In Telluride, the questioning of Duncan was kept up all day and he stoutly kept to the original story that he had told. He said that he had never known Otis or Herbert McDaniels before the ill-fated trip from Glenwood Springs. Duncan said he had made whiskey during prohibition (but for that matter, who didn't?) but he had never sold any to the Indians as that was a federal offense. He said that Otis may have worked at the sheep camp but Duncan didn't know all of the men that were up there. If Otis worked there it was as a total stranger and just someone who had been hired for a short time. Deputy Duncan said he had never been to a dance with Otis and as far as dating the same girl, as Otis claimed, the only possibility would have to have been that somehow Otis knew Fern Barrett whom Duncan had occasionally dated.

Duncan did admit buying a candy bar for the prisoners but that certainly wasn't aiding an escape. He stoutly denied ever doing any talking with the prisoners and only loosened the shackles enough to relieve excess tightness when the prisoners complained so lustily about the heat and sweat galling their legs. Duncan also made it quite clear at this point that he was not wearing a holster and did not have a gun of any kind at any time during the trip. He stated that he was on the streets of Cortez one day when Sheriff Dunlap hailed him and asked him if he would like to take a little trip to drive the car for him and to act in the capacity of deputy sheriff. He said that Dunlap had a revolver and there was a shotgun in the back of the front seat under a blanket. Those were all the guns that he knew of.

District Attorney Haywood was not completely satisfied with Lem Duncan's story and decided to hold him for complicity in the murder of Dunlap and take him to the jail at Grand Junction where he could be brought face to face with the McDaniels boys. Sheriff Warrick went to Grand Junction with Haywood to sign the information charging Duncan with complicity in the murder of Dunlap. Haywood's main point in filing this charge was that Duncan made no move whatsoever to help Dunlap when he was being shot by Otis McDaniels. But we should remember that Otis had a revolver with four bullets left in it. He had just killed one man and probably wouldn't hesitate to kill Duncan should he have tried to make a grab for the shotgun lying covered by a blanket in the front seat. Very few men are foolhardy enough to try something as risky as that. The district attorney seemed to have been swayed by the testimony of both the McDaniels brothers.

When they reached the Grand Junction jail, Jess Robinson, sheriff of Montezuma County, was at the jail conferring with Otis McDaniels. During the conversation Robinson became enraged at some of the remarks coming from Otis and called him a "dirty, rotten liar," and reached through the bars and grabbed Otis by the throat and was well on his way to choking him to death when Haywood grabbed Robinson from behind, tore him loose from the throat of Otis, and threw him bodily out into the hall. Then Sheriff Lumley, who was in another room and heard the disturbance, came on the scene and was of a very strong mind to jail Robinson.

Guy Warrick signed the information for Haywood but he was sick at heart at having to do it. So much was based on the testimony of a man who had committed two murders and Lem Duncan had a clean record and had only signed on for the job to be helpful to Sheriff Wesley Dunlap. That night Warrick returned to Telluride with the wife and father of Duncan and placed them in a hotel for the remainder of the night. The next day Warrick met with District Attorney W. F. Haywood in Montrose and removed his name from the information that he had

Guy Warrick (shown here with his wife, Viola) served two terms as the sheriff of San Miguel County.

Courtesy of Eileen Brown

BOOK TWO: The McDaniels Brothers and the Westfall/Dunlap Murders ❈ 101

signed. After suffering this setback, Haywood called James Noland in Durango and told him he could have the McDaniels brothers for trial first for the murder of James Westfall. San Miguel County would pass up its chance to have the prisoners first for trial on the Dunlap murder. Haywood needed some more time to try to bring a murder charge against Deputy Sheriff Lem Duncan. Lem Duncan returned to Cortez after District Attorney Haywood of Grand Junction could find no one willing to sign the information charging the deputy with complicity in the slaying and escape.

Duncan had been held in Telluride about five days during which time he answered the questioning of the district attorney's staff and reenacted the events that took place in the San Miguel canyon on the morning of July 15. During the investigation, Duncan was in the custody of Sheriff Guy Warrick of Telluride who could find nothing in the way of evidence against him so did not comply with the district attorney's request for a signed information charging Duncan with murder along with the McDaniels brothers. Duncan stated that his treatment by the sheriff showed a fine spirit of fairness that was never swayed by the implications of the two men who shot Sheriff Dunlap and made their escape.

People in Montezuma County generally agreed that the implication of Duncan by the McDaniels brothers was a trick on their part to befuddle the issue and they were afraid that if the case went before a jury in that condition, it might win a lighter sentence than their crime deserved. Several offers of aid were advanced but the release of Duncan, of course, made them unnecessary.

The two notorious prisoners were taken to Durango on Tuesday, August 13. Responsibility for their safekeeping after the surprise demand for them early Tuesday morning by Sheriff Jess Robinson of Cortez, was placed entirely with District Attorney James Noland of Durango by Governor Edwin C. Johnson. Repeated warnings of a lynching should the men be returned to southwestern Colorado had been heard. The belief was rapidly growing that the men had been taken back to Cortez and Durango to be hanged by the angry crowds. District Attorney Noland denied this and declared, "There will not be anything like that. Every precaution is being taken. The prisoners will not go to Cortez, but will be spirited to Durango, arraigned and rushed to the state prison at Canon City for safekeeping."

Sheriff Jess Robinson and Deputies Fred West and Fred Medford accompanied the prisoners to Durango in as quiet a manner as possible. They did attract a small crowd at a cafe in Silverton where they stopped to eat. The handcuffs and shackles were removed on the sidewalk in front of the eating place among a crowd of curious spectators. After the meal, the prisoners were re-handcuffed and shackled together again and the trip continued on to Durango. They arrived at the courthouse at 4:30 p.m.. and were quickly taken to the office of District Judge J. B. O'Rourke, where they were arraigned on charges of first degree murder in the "starvation death" of aged rancher James Westfall. The McDaniels brothers pleaded "not guilty." Efforts to keep their presence in Durango a secret had been successful, and at 5:45 p.m., with the addition of Indian Agent Frank Weaver, the group proceeded on their way to the Canon City prison for the safekeeping of the prisoners until their trial, which had been set for September 10. Attorneys S. W. Carpenter of Mancos and John J. Downey of Cortez were appointed by the court to defend the pair of murderers.

It had also been reported to Governor Johnson that the prisoners were being returned to Durango by the same sheriff who attacked Otis McDaniels in his cell and had him by the throat, screaming "you are a dirty, rotten liar." The Governor said he appreciated being advised on the matter and he proposed to get in touch with District Attorney Noland; that regardless of how guilty these men were, they were entitled to a fair trial; that he wanted no discredit brought on the state by any attempted lynching; and that he was putting the entire responsibility onto District Attorney Noland to see that the men were adequately protected. This message was quickly passed on, with forceful emphasis, to Sheriff Jess Robinson.

18: The Trial

¶ The McDaniels court case came to trial as scheduled on September 10 and the jury was selected the first day. Three panels of veniremen were exhausted before the selection of jurors was completed. The crowded little courtroom was tense on September 11 as the state again resumed its case against the McDaniels brothers. The state won an important point in its case when the court ruled, after hearing prosecution arguments without the jury present, that the confessions of both Otis and Herbert relative to the robbery and binding of James Westfall, which resulted in his death, were admissible as evidence.

In the closing hours of the trial, District Attorney James Noland asked for the death penalty for Otis and life imprisonment for Herbert. Noland accused Otis of being the perpetrator of the crime. The case was presented and argued and witnesses were brought forth to testify. By mid-afternoon the case was given to the jury. After six hours of deliberation Wednesday night, the verdict of "guilty as charged" was brought in at 10:25 p.m. When court resumed Thursday morning, September 12, District Judge J. B. O'Rourke, upon the request of Noland, delayed imposing sentence in order that San Miguel County could file murder charges against the pair for the slaying of Sheriff W. W. Dunlap of Cortez.

Not satisfied with the verdict of the jury in Durango District Court that found the McDaniels brothers guilty but did not recommend the death penalty for either, District Attorney Haywood of Grand Junction filed charges of first degree murder against both men and asked that they be transported immediately to the jail in that city Thursday night. A tentative date for the trial was set for October 14, 1935. It had been understood between the two district attorneys before the trial in Durango that if the death penalty was not secured there, they would be tried for the murder of Sheriff Dunlap at Telluride.

The recommended sentence at Durango was a surprise, not only to the prosecution, but to the defense attorneys and the brothers themselves. It was reported that after the trial when an attorney for the McDaniels rose to make the usual motion for a new trial, Otis pulled him back into the chair and asked him to not say any more as he was as satisfied as he might be. As the clerk of the district court read the jury's decision, a smile spread across Otis McDaniel's face and shortly afterward he said, "I sure am lucky but Herbert got more than he deserved." Both brothers seemed happy with the verdict and from their attitude and statements, they evidently believed they had been virtually sitting in the two chairs in the gas chamber and then by some miracle were given a new lease on life. To Otis a life sentence may have meant that every year that began offered another three hundred and sixty five chances to engineer an escape.

The McDaniels brothers were taken to Telluride early Monday morning, September 16 for arraignment before District Judge Straud M. Logan. They were accompanied by Sheriff Lumley and Chief of Police Decker of Grand Junction. They were joined in Montrose by Sheriff McAnally and at Ridgway by Sheriff Jess Wood of Ouray. District Attorney W. F. Haywood and District Judge S. M. Logan preceded them there on Sunday afternoon. The brothers were formally charged with the murder, on July 15, of Sheriff Wesley W. Dunlap of Montezuma County. They pleaded "not guilty." Judge Logan appointed Lawrence Bothwell of Grand Junction to defend them.

Because Attorney Bothwell desired to have easy access to them in order to work up the case for trial October 14, he asked that they be left in the Grand Junction jail. Judge Logan ruled they could be left there for one week, after which they would be taken to Telluride and turned over to the San Miguel County sheriff. After their arraignment the brothers were taken by the sheriff to the scene of the crime near Placerville, where a hunt was to made for the guns which they lost during their travels after the shooting of Dunlap.

19: The Second Trial

Otis and Herbert McDaniels, convicted slayers of James Westfall and already under the shadow of life imprisonment in the state penitentiary, went on trial for the murder of Sheriff Dunlap on Monday, October 14 in the San Miguel District Court, Judge Strand M. Logan presiding. The trial was held in the historic old courthouse in Telluride. The District Attorney was going all out for a death sentence for the two murderers. By late Monday afternoon the court had accepted a jury of twelve men but the defense excused two of them. Another panel of prospective jurors had to be rounded up for the selection of the last two. The wives of the two men on trial were present in the courtroom as well as a few relatives.

Tuesday morning, October 15, the prosecution presented its case to the court. Numerous witnesses were called and Lem Duncan was the last to testify for the prosecution. He told the same story, in every detail, that he told in the beginning. He was cross-examined for over two hours by the defense attorney but did not vary from his original testimony. The prosecution had Otis McDaniels on the stand for about two hours also. Otis had changed his testimony on several points but he said that the previous statements were not made under oath and were not signed. He claimed that force was used to extract the information from him. He maintained that fifteen officers had surrounded him and that he was beaten and did not know what he was saying.

District Attorney Noland, Sheriff Lumley, Chief of Police Decker and officer Fred Weaver were put on the stand as rebuttal witnesses and all testified that what Otis claimed had not happened and was totally false. Otis also admitted that he had lied about Duncan, and District Attorney Haywood had him so confused that he could not remember how to repeat his several concocted stories about the murder of Sheriff Dunlap.

Otis was the only witness for the defense. While Haywood had him on the stand for cross-examination, he was forced to admit that he had been sentenced to prison in Utah for fifteen to twenty years and to a similar term in New Mexico before the Westfall slaying. He served a short time on each and was paroled. It was obvious to all that nothing he had to say could be believed. Several people in the courtroom were heard to remark that it looked to them like Lem Duncan was more on trial than the McDaniels brothers.

20: The Second Verdict

¶ The jury got the case at 12:20 p.m. Thursday October 17 after almost twelve hours of delay because of the disagreement between the attorneys over what the instructions to the jurors should be. They finally got it straightened out at 10:30 a.m. Friday and then the jurors were advised as to their choice of verdicts and the punishment that goes with each. The jury discussed the case until 3:00 a.m. Friday morning, at which time they reached a verdict. They were then sequestered by the bailiff until court opened at 9:00 a.m. at which time the verdict was handed over to the court. The packed courtroom was hushed in expectancy of the verdict. It came as a surprise to no one. GUILTY OF MURDER IN THE FIRST DEGREE. Recommended sentences were death for Otis in the gas chamber at the state penitentiary at Canon City, Colorado, and life imprisonment for Herbert with no recommendation for parole.

As was expected, the attorney for the defense excepted to the verdict and requested, and received, a ten-day period in which to file for a new trial. Sentencing was thereby delayed ten days, although it would follow the recommendations of the jury: death for Otis and life for Herbert. Attorney Lawrence Bothwell filed a motion for a new trial for Otis who received the death sentence. He did not ask for a new trial for Herbert, who was given life in prison. On Thursday, October 31, Judge Logan denied the motion for a new trial for Otis and sentenced him to die in the lethal gas chamber at Canon City during the week of February 15, 1936.

The verdict of the jury had been upheld. Otis's lawyer was allowed nine days in which to prepare a bill of exceptions and appeal to the state supreme court. In spite of having given this allotted time to the defense lawyer, Judge Logan set the date for the execution of Otis. In order that the court not leave any loopholes in the case, it was decided that San Miguel County Sheriff Guy Warrick would take the prisoners to Durango to the court of Judge J. B. O'Rourke and have him pass sentence on the pair for the "starvation murder" of James Westfall. Sheriff Warrick delivered the prisoners to the court in Durango but upon his arrival there he found out that Judge O'Rourke was not in town and someone in authority told him that it didn't matter if the pair were sentenced there or not. Sheriff Warrick returned to Telluride with his prisoners.

Meanwhile, it seems, when the brothers were sentenced in Telluride on Thursday, it was discovered the court records did not possess any mittimus blanks for such cases. It was arranged that District Attorney Haywood would return to Grand Junction, prepare the mittimus papers, mail them special delivery to Sheriff McAnally in Montrose, and Sheriff Warrick would stop there for them on his way to Canon City with the prisoners. All went well and the papers arrived about the same time as Sheriff Warrick. Before the papers were turned over to Warrick he was told that instructions had come from District Attorney Haywood, District Attorney Noland and others that Sheriff Warrick must turn around and deliver his prisoners to the court in Durango for sentencing there. The messages were very forceful and didn't leave any room for personal opinions.

Sheriff Warrick turned around and for the second time in twenty-four hours, delivered his prisoners to the court in Durango. Sheriff Warrick was very good-natured about the whole mixed up procedure and remarked that he hoped he didn't wear out the prisoners carrying out the diverse and sundry orders of the law. He still hoped to have the pair of murderers in Canon City by Saturday.

It is probably without parallel in state legal records that two brothers have ever been convicted and sentenced for two murders through two trials. It was an unusual procedure which has taxed the expertise of the legal fraternity so as to leave no technical loopholes for appeals and unnecessary delay in carrying out the sentences. In the event that any technicalities might arise to invalidate the sentences in the Dunlap murder case, the authorities would have the sentences in the Westfall case to fall back upon.

21: The Execution

Monday, February 10, 1936: The word from Canon City stated that although Otis McDaniels was still hopeful the state's plan to hand him a St. Valentine' day present of death might miscarry, the state was going ahead with plans for his execution Friday night. His chances for evasion of the death penalty were very slim. There were two possibilities: one was an appeal to the state supreme court — the other, a very doubtful one, was an appeal to Governor Edwin C. Johnson to commute the sentence to life imprisonment.

Wednesday, February 12, 1936: Otis still seemed unconcerned about his impending death. He seemed sure that there would be no attempts to save his life and his greatest concern seemed to be whether or not he would be baptized in time. He was converted to the Catholic religion a few days before.

On the previous Saturday, Warden Best allowed the two brothers to talk for thirty minutes. The visit between the brothers took place in the prison interview room with a guard listening in on the conversation. Neither mentioned Otis's impending death in the gas chamber and little was said of their prison life. Instead, they talked of more pleasant things — of when the two were children together in the San Juan country where they were raised and spent practically their entire lives. They talked of their parents, of cow-punching experiences, of many things, but never of the rendezvous that Otis must keep. They smiled and they joked. For half an hour Otis forgot such things as hydrocyanic gas, prison bars and death. Then the interview was over and the prisoners returned to their cells and reality. Here Otis spent most of his time reading the Bible and other religious tracts that were available to him.

February 14, 1936: The strain of waiting execution in the gas chamber was beginning to tell on Otis McDaniels who had so far been a man of steel nerves. After spending a restless night he called for his religious adviser, Father Albert, at dawn. His only request in the way of a menu was for a drink of whiskey which was denied by prison officials. Then Warden Best asked if there was anything else that Otis might want. "Yes, Warden, it's about Herb — my brother." He was with Otis at the two killings. In fact it was to get money so Herbert might marry a sixteen-year-old girl, that they bound and robbed old Jim Westfall and left him in his home near Lewis, Colorado, to die of starvation. "Please let Herb be with me the last days. He's loyal and true blue, Warden, and he'll make a good prisoner. You won't have any trouble with him — he promised me that. He'll stay put. You can trust him and my last wish is that you do. I want to sort of feel that Herbert will get out before he is an old man. I am thirteen years older than he is and I led him into all his trouble. Just tell me you'll give Herbert a break and let me answer all the letters I've got—the one to my wife especially—and I'll not ask anything else."

Otis cried when he talked of Herbert and he made an earnest plea to the warden that Herbert might eventually be educated a little and taught a trade so that if ever he did get out of prison he could support himself in a legitimate way. "We never gave Herbert much of a chance. We just let him run wild and he never got much training or education."

Then Otis spoke of his wife, alone on wind-swept Red Mesa, just north of the New Mexico line — the mesa where McDaniels lived. "I had a letter from her yesterday," he told the guards. "She's all alone down there on the mesa now. It used to be that while I was running around she lived with her folks. But lately — well, she's been alone. She's on relief. She wanted to come to see me but she couldn't get the money for the trip. She wanted to take my case to the Supreme Court but that was out of the question."

At 7:45 p.m. Otis courageously walked to the gas chamber with Warden Roy Best and Father Schaller, the prison chaplain who had converted him to the Catholic faith. Dr. R. E. Holmes pronounced him dead at 8:01 p.m., fourteen minutes after he entered the room. Otis McDaniels was the fiftieth person to be executed for murder within the walls of the Colorado prison. The population of "Woodpecker Hill", the prison burial ground, was increased by one as Otis's body was lowered into the frozen ground.

BOOK THREE:
The Hidden Treasure of the McCarty Gang

1: Three Cowboys

On or about June 26, 1889, three dust-caked riders on jaded mounts rode into the roundup camp and asked if they could have a meal and rest their horses. The horses were near exhaustion and showed plainly all the signs of having been pushed to the limit, ridden hard enough to outdistance any posse or Colorado sheriff that might have taken their trail. In Utah they would be safe until Colorado authorities had time to notify the Utah law officers to be on the watch for them. The roundup crew was a little short on cowboys so the wagon boss asked the men if they would like to work until the roundup was finished in about mid-July. They all agreed they would work awhile but advised the boss not to be surprised if they had to ask for their wages and leave on short notice.

No one in the roundup camp had been to town or seen a newspaper since the roundup started and they did not know that three men had robbed the Bank of Telluride, Colorado, on June 24, 1889. The robbers had staked a change of horses out about twenty miles south of Telluride and on these fresh mounts they were easily able to outdistance the posse that had taken their trail. The tired mounts were turned loose but one of them refused to be left behind. Tom McCarty's white race mare "Suzy," known all over southwestern Colorado, took their trail and endeavored to keep on going, although several miles behind. The Telluride posse had stopped at the relay point, knowing full well they could never catch the bank robbers on their fresh mounts. Their horses were already tired so they gathered up the horses left by the outlaws and returned to Telluride. The sheriff rode the brown colt that belonged to "Bud" Parker for several years while he made his rounds of the Telluride night spots.

That evening the bank robbers made it to the Aztec Springs Ranch owned by Tom McCarty, the leader of the gang, a few miles out of Mancos, Colorado. The next day a stable hand at a livery store in Mancos overheard two deputies talking of someone having seen a white horse that showed all the signs of having been ridden very hard. She was in a state of severe exhaustion and bleeding from the nose. She was "trailing up" along the route used by the Telluride bank robbers as they made their way along the Dolores River below Rico. Anyone who saw her would know she was McCarty's pet race mare as she had a reputation of being unbeatable in a race.

As quickly as he could leave town without causing suspicion the stable hand rode out to the McCarty ranch and informed the three men of what he had overheard. The robbers knew the deputies would put two and two together and feared they might already be on their way to arrest them. Bud Parker, later known as Butch Cassidy, snapped at Tom McCarty saying, "I told you not to ride that white mare. Now everybody in southwestern Colorado will know who we are." The three bank robbers hurriedly saddled their mounts, stuffed a few cold biscuits and extra cartridges into their saddle bags and left the ranch at a rapid pace. By circuitous routes they made their way west towards the sanctuary of the Utah border about seventy-five miles distant. That same evening they rode into the roundup camp.

2: A Hide Out and a Holdup

Having tired of the everyday work of a cowboy the three bank robbers left the area. Matt Warner went farther west into Utah. Bud Parker stayed in the Moab, Utah vicinity, until he came up with a name change. He knew by then that the three Telluride bank robbers had been identified by name. Too many people who had seen them leaving Telluride knew them personally. He decided that it would be a wise move to go by another name. He had worked one time for a horse rancher named Mike Cassidy and he had liked him quite well. He also liked the name Cassidy. As a matter of fact the short stay of Parker in the Wyoming penitentiary was for stealing horses to help increase the herd of Mike

Cassidy. Bud Parker had also worked one time as a butcher for a meat market in Ophir, Colorado, owned by Jack Elliott, and had frequently been called "Butch" as short for butcher. The two names went together with a pleasing sound and from then on Bud Parker was known as Butch Cassidy.

James O. Miller of Collbran, Colorado did this painting of Robert Leroy Parker, later known as "Butch Cassidy."
Courtesy of James O. Miller

A current day photograph of the McCarty hideout. The dark hole in the rock was used for saddle and tack storage by Tom McCarty in the winter of 1890.

Photo by Tom Bradford. Courtesy of Bob and Ann Riley

Tom McCarty returned to Paradox, Colorado and to the ranch of his brother Bill. In a few days' time he secluded himself under a rimrock overhang on Hideout Mesa above La Sal Creek. The mesa was given that name after the winter that Tom McCarty spent there. He spent most of his time improving the hideout as a place to live. One end was closed off with hewn cedar poles, dovetailed at the ends for a better fit. The other end was sealed with a rock wall creating one large room. A fireplace was built out front so that smoke would not fill the living quarters. McCarty presumably did his cooking at night so that smoke would not be visible to any curious person who might be in the area.

The open side of the McCarty hideout faces southeast. The rock structure is a fireplace and cooking unit.
Photo by Tom Bradford. Courtesy of Bob and Ann Riley

Also since no sign of a trash dump was found, it is presumed that when his brother Bill brought him groceries that he also packed his trash out in the empty panniers and hauled it miles away to further secure the secrecy of the hideout. To keep the hideout as secret as possible no one ventured near it and they only packed in groceries when a storm was brewing and they knew that fresh snow would cover their tracks. The hideout was cleverly hidden and the mesa itself was very difficult to find. More people in recent years have stumbled upon it than those who were actually searching for it. A number of people in the last thirty years have been lucky enough to be led right to it while chasing a mountain lion with hounds. As with Tom McCarty the lions found it to be a good escape route.

The west end of the living area of the McCarty hideout was a rock wall. Tom McCarty was never known to be a stone mason.

Photo by Tom Bradford. Courtesy of Bob and Ann Riley

The hideout was so close to the Utah-Colorado border that should a Utah sheriff discover an occupant, if he had any warning at all the occupant could dodge his way down through the rimrock and trees and be in Colorado very quickly. A Utah sheriff could not touch him there. The reverse of this unique location was also true since if trouble came from Colorado he would already be in Utah with the Outlaw Trail only a few miles away. There were always outlaws riding this route from Idaho to Arizona and no sheriff was ever known to venture into the Outlaw Trail.

It was at this hideout that the McCarty brothers, Tom and Bill, during their visits each grocery trip that winter, made plans to rob the Farmers and Merchants Bank of Delta, Colorado. Tom's youngest brother, "Ekky," was working on the Maxwell Ranch in Paradox Valley breaking horses. He knew that Tom had lost Suzy and he was in the process of breaking a white gelding for his brother. He would also be called "Suzy." Ekky was very special to Tom and he spent long hours talking to Ekky about living the straight life. Tom had never allowed Ekky to go on any of their robberies. He loved him very much and didn't want him to live the same life that Tom had chosen. For that reason Ekky was not included in the group that set out for Delta. It nearly broke Ekky's heart to have to stay when he learned that Bill's son Fred, younger than Ekky, was allowed to make the trip. Bill and Tom thought Fred might come in handy for holding the horses while they went into the bank.

The east end of the living area of the McCarty hideout was a wall of cedar poles. Note how they dovetailed the ends of the poles for a better fit.

Photo by Tom Bradford. Courtesy of Bob and Ann Riley

On September 6, 1893, with his brother Bill and Bill's son Fred, Tom McCarty staged the ill-fated holdup of the Farmers And Merchants Bank of Delta. The McCartys had been in town for several days and had been running their horses up and down the alleys of the town daily. A curious resident asked them what they were doing and they told him that a big race was coming up soon and they were conditioning their horses. What they were really doing was getting the lay of the land and getting the horses acquainted with the escape route out of town for the day when they would rob the bank. The robbery was staged and the bandits got out of the bank with two sacks of loot carried by Bill. Young Fred got trigger happy and shot and killed the cashier and the sound of the shot was what alerted the residents of the town that all was not well at the bank. Bill McCarty stuffed the sacks of money into his saddle bags and Tom helped hold the anxious horses while Fred and his dad mounted and then they all started down the alley in a swift run.

This photo of Fred McCarty, the son of Bill McCarty, was taken shortly after he was killed robbing the Farmers and Merchant's Bank in Delta.

Courtesy of P. David Smith

Bill McCarty's body had to be propped up for this postmortem photo. Gratefully someone put a hat on his badly damaged head.

Courtesy of P. David Smith

Across the street from the bank was a hardware store run by a man named Ray Simpson. Upon hearing the shot in the bank he picked up a .44 caliber Sharps rifle and walked out into the street where he had a view of the alley behind the bank. He saw the men mount their horses and start down the alley. He fired once and Bill McCarty tumbled from his saddle with a bullet hole in his head. His son Fred whirled his horse around and came racing back to see if he could be of any help to his dad. He leaned down to get a better look at Bill lying there in the alley. Fred's head was about even with his horse's neck. Simpson fired again and Fred fell from his horse, shot through the head. The bullet passed on through his head and into the neck of the horse severing the jugular vein. The horse staggered out into main street and fell dead. Simpson fired another shot at the rapidly disappearing Tom McCarty. The bullet struck Suzy in the heel of a hind hoof. The horse stumbled and almost fell but with amazing agility stayed on his feet.

A little known fact about the escape of the lone survivor was that just as Suzy was shot in the heel Bill McCarty's horse came up alongside Tom's mount running at full speed and Tom made a flying leap onto his back. Bill's saddle bags had all the loot from the robbery and Tom made good his escape by outrunning a posse for over twenty miles. For the next several days he eluded the law by spending most of his time in and around Sinbad Valley and the rugged and eroded hideouts of "Sew-Um-Up" Mesa. He spent one night in Sinbad Valley with his shirt tail relative Gene Grimes, the lone hand cattle rustler of "Sew-Um-Up" Mesa. In a few more days Tom was in Moab, Utah where he was welcomed by friends and relatives. He swore then he would never take another kid along on a bank robbery.

A Mrs. Hendrickson, living near Sinbad, told the story to a friend of mine that Tom McCarty had $38,000.00 with him when he rode into Sinbad. The cabin where he stayed a couple of days was about half-way up on the south side of Sinbad Valley. There were notches cut into the logs that formed the walls where a rifle barrel could be placed and every switchback of the trail up from the bottom could be covered with rifle fire. Mrs. Hendrickson also told my friend that Tom McCarty didn't have that money with him when he rode out of Sinbad. Actually, I doubt very seriously that she saw him leave. According to Gene Grimes, Tom got up and left in the middle of the night, making his way out of the head of Sinbad, through Kirk's Basin to the head of Deep Creek and thence over Geyser Pass and down to Moab where he had friends and a chance to rest up a little. The stories circulated about Tom McCarty's money have brought numerous fortune hunters to Sinbad Valley but all for naught.

James O. Miller of Collbran, Colorado drew his conception of Tom McCarty in his later years.
Courtesy of James O. Miller

Soon after resting up in Moab, Tom found his way to Oregon where his brother Bill owned property and another brother, George, was living. With his narrow escape from the law and after suffering the loss of his brother and nephew, Tom's arrival in Oregon marked the beginning of a new life. He set out to live a proper life and began his quest by purchasing breeding stock and operating a large horse ranch which was on some property of his brother's. One thing the McCartys did right was to raise good horses. The one Tom made his escape on from Delta was truly a magnificent animal.

3: Buried Treasure

Ekky McCarty, thinking it might be a wise move on his part to leave the area where his brothers had committed their bank robbing activities, took leave of his job breaking horses for the Maxwell Ranch and left the Paradox Valley for quite a few years. He roamed the western states, working as a cowboy wherever work could be found, until he found himself in Oregon and once again with his brothers Tom and George. Here he remained for several years in perfect peace and contentment — that is, until his brother Tom drew him a map. After that his life was just a period of restlessness of looking forward to the day when he would return to Colorado and dig up the buried loot of the McCarty gang.

Along in the 1920s, after World War I was over and the boys had all come home from France and resumed their lives, Ekky McCarty showed up in Paradox Valley. Things there were very different than when he had left it. True, the valley looked the same. The beautiful red rock walls were still there. The springs still flowed cold and clear. Pastures were full of livestock and the whole valley seemed to be at peace with the world. Still, a lot was missing. Maxwell had sold his ranch and moved away. There wasn't a person in the valley that Ekky knew. One thing he remembered well was that he had a cousin named Vere Ray who lived in the Naturita area, twenty-five miles east of Paradox. Ekky made his way to that place and found his cousin.

The youngest of the McCarty boys had a plan and he wanted to share it with someone. He was in possession of Tom McCarty's crudely drawn map showing where the money was hidden that the McCarty gang had buried along the banks of Tabeguache Creek. They didn't want to go into the town of Delta to rob a bank with $3000.00 in their saddle bags so they rolled it into an oilskin slicker, stuffed that into a heavy leather saddle bag and buried it on a dry-looking bench of ground that was back a fair distance from the creek bank. Their plan was to retrieve it on their return trip from robbing the Farmers and Merchants Bank. The plans they had for Delta had, of course, gone terribly awry. After the holdup in Delta, Tom had given up going back to the buried money as deputies from Delta could easily track their horses back to that point. After all, he had all the loot that his brother Bill had stuffed into his saddle bags.

Vere Ray and Ekky McCarty labored over the map for some time trying to figure out the part of Tabeguache Basin that the map indicated. Vere Ray had been a cowboy in that area all of his life and he thought that if anyone could ever find that hidden loot, he could. Ekky thought the same way and the next day they were on horses and headed up into the first of several areas they planned to search. The map showed a small stretch of crooked stream bank and the presence of two large pine trees. It was five steps south of one tree and eleven steps east from the other where the X was on the map. A full day's search produced absolutely nothing in the way of encouragement for the two men.

The country had been logged over in recent years and no large pine trees were to be found. Lots of fences had been built, and in some places ground had been cleared and homesteaded. The creek had flooded and changed course many times and in places was so completely grown up with willows that the banks were hardly visible. Still, the searchers kept on looking for any kind of a clue, but it was not forthcoming. Up to that point they had not stuck a shovel into the ground. After three days they decided it was fruitless to look any more. Ekky McCarty went back to Oregon and Vere Ray resumed his life as cowboy and rancher. He still had a perfect picture of the map engraved in his mind and planned to some day take another look around along the banks of Tabeguache Creek.

One day, while visiting with his friend Emerson Williams, Vere Ray mentioned the map and what it stood for and how he came to know all he did about the buried money. This conversation really got the attention of Williams as he, like Ray, was a cowboy who had spent his entire life riding that range. They decided to spend a day or two in that area and see what they might turn up.

They never found a spot that even remotely resembled the map. Too many years had passed and too many things had changed. They looked far up the creek and far down it and a hundred places in between but it was all the same sad story. They went home in disgust but smarter about looking for buried treasure. It's still there, somewhere. Might be turned to dust by now. It's only been something like 105 years ago.

It is interesting to note that all the horses that Tom McCarty turned loose were gathered by Uncompahgre Plateau cowboys and returned to the Maxwell Ranch. Suzy completely recovered from the heel wound and was also returned to the Maxwell Ranch, probably the only good thing to come out of that fateful Delta trip.

As for Butch Cassidy, the following article was written by Harry B. Adsit, former employer of Cassidy, for the *Dolores Star* February 11, 1938.

> In the year 1888, I was the proud possessor of five thousand head of well bred cattle and two thousand head of range horses. My range was located on one of the tributaries of the San Miguel River in San Miguel County, Colorado. My main camp was at the base of what was known as the "Lone Cone," a circular dome over twelve thousand feet high and twenty miles in circumference. Its sides up to the timberline furnished wonderful feed for our stock and enabled me to ship a trainload of fat cattle and another of horses to the market in Omaha, Nebraska and St. Louis, Missouri. Our nearest supply point, forty miles distant, was the mining town of Telluride and the mines of this section furnished a market for our beef. We shipped our surplus horses by the train load to the above mentioned markets. There was always an open season on mavericks or un-branded horses and I recall that in one train load I shipped one hundred and thirty head of mavericks.
>
> Our range covered a vast area of thirty miles square lying between the San Miguel and Dolores Rivers. There were only a dozen cow outfits in this territory — it was a game paradise and for years we never killed a beef steer,

subsisting entirely on the game we killed. The happiest ten years of my life were passed on this range — wild horses, wild cattle and game.

Two boys rode up to the ranch one day and asked for work. When asked what they could do, they stated their specialty was breaking broncos. I told them we would round up twenty-five head of three and four-year-olds and that they could go to work. One of the boys was Butch Cassidy — his real name I will not mention, as his family is well known in southern Utah. Their work demonstrated that they were experts on riding and breaking horses and they continued their work for a year.

The horses that developed speed and intelligence we would keep for the cow outfit — the dead-heads we would ship and those that would not stop bucking we would save for Buffalo Bill's Wild West circus, for which there was a standing offer of $150.00 a head. Occasionally we would use the boys on the beef herd and Butch developed an uncanny ability in handling beef and I would take him with me when driving a bunch to Telluride for the mines. The Tomboy and Smuggler Union Mines would each hang up a hundred head every fall for winter consumption. On these trips I discovered that this boy had a personality—above the average in height, good features, sandy hair, piercing eyes and rapid fire way of talking which later served him well, he cared not at all for liquor or cards, although he occasionally held the candle while the boys played poker on a saddle blanket in the open.

As we lay in our blankets gazing up at the big white stars in this high altitude he would declare that he would make a mark in this world — and he did. When their year expired Butch stated they wanted to visit their folks in Utah. I told them to go into the pasture and select two of the best four-year-olds they had recently broken and accept them with my compliments. I gave them a check and told them to come back soon.

Two weeks later, I was riding into Telluride and my two

trained collies were with me. As I rode up Keystone hill, I looked up the road and saw four men approaching on the run. As they neared me, I recognized two boys. I shouted, "What's up." They replied, "Haven't got time to talk. Adios!" Butch had lost his hat. As I continued my way wondering at their delay in going home, I looked up and saw a mile away, a posse approaching. I knew it was a posse as I could see the sun glisten from the Winchesters. "Did you see them?" the sheriff asked. "Yes", I replied.

He then summoned me as a member of the posse. He said, "You have a fresh horse and here's a Winchester, now lead out." I asked what they had done. He replied that they had held up the San Miguel Valley Bank. The posse was made up of clerks and others that could not ride well in a covered wagon, but as I turned to lead out, a gambler, a former cowboy, rode alongside and told me the story. He said no one had been killed or injured, that one of the boys had shot at the feet of the cashier to make him stand still — that the shot had started his mount bucking and he never saw such bucking or such riding. The horse bucked his hat off. That was Butch and it would have been embarrassing had he been thrown.

The posse was far behind us and as we crossed the San Miguel on their trail I noted they had left the main trail into the timber. I pulled up my horse and told my friend that unless he wanted to die, we had better stop for awhile, that I was a pretty fair shot as well as the boys and if we tangled up with them it would mean several funerals. I inferred the boys had gone to their camp for a change of horses or food. We remained still for probably half an hour, then ambled slowly up the trail — and soon discovered where they had returned to the trail. In a short time we met L. L. Nunn, the president of the bank, and when informed his bank had been robbed, he said, "What shall I do?" I told him I had ridden my horse forty miles and as he had a fresh horse, I would suggest we change.

Shortly after we changed, I saw the boys riding down the side of the mountain towards the Ames power plant. We followed down and at Trout Lake we were informed that they had just passed, shooting as they went and if we speeded up we would overtake them. I thought we were going too fast and slowed up. As we passed a stage station, I asked the tender, whom I knew, if he would put my dogs in the grain room and feed them until I returned — that I did not want to run them to death.

We finally reached the head of the West Dolores where we found they had divided the money, $500 and $1000 wrappers lying on the ground. Our horses were grazing as the sheriff came poking along. He was not an aggressive wild west officer. In fact, as the old darkey said about his dog, "He was a little bit slow on 'possum and not quite fast enough for coon." The sheriff at once ordered me to take two men to Rico, remount and cross the Johnny Bull range, in the hope we would head them off on the Dolores. This was agreeable to me, as we were taking two sides of a triangle whereas the sheriff could follow straight down the Dolores.

We reached the Dolores ahead of the sheriff and found that the boys had passed down the trail ahead of us. In half an hour the sheriff appeared and asked what we were going to do. I told him I had changed horses three times, had covered a hundred miles at top speed and we were exhausted and going to sleep. He said he would poke along to the mesa. It was then dark; the month of June, the grass belly-deep to the horses. We unsaddled, hobbled our horses and laid down on our saddle blankets and as the Dolores found its way over the rocks and around the bends on its way to the mighty Colorado, we were soon lulled to sleep.

Some time in the night I was awakened by some animal licking my face. As I raised up, my two collies jumped all over me with evident delight. They had escaped from the grain room, had followed me thirty miles after a dozen horsemen had covered my tracks. They were seen near Rico running with their heads in the air — I am told collies do not track like hounds, but take the scent from the air. The sheriff returned at daylight next morning, leading the dappled brown colt I had given Butch. He found him on the mesa, almost dead from exhaustion. We all started our return trip picking up our exchange horses enroute. Ten days later I received a letter from Butch which ran as follows: "Dear Harry: I understand the sheriff of San Miguel County is riding the dapple brown colt you gave me. I want you to tell Mr. Sheriff that this horse packed me one hundred and ten miles in ten hours across that broken country and declared a dividend of $22,580 and this will be your order for the horse. Please send him over to me at Moab, Utah, at the first opportunity."

I handed the letter to the sheriff and demanded the horse as it carried my brand. It was well known all over three counties. I suggested that he go to Moab and get his men. He refused my demand and claimed that as I had given the horse to Butch, it no longer belonged to me, and as the bank and the county refused to put up any more money, he would keep the horse to help pay his expenses. He also claimed the horse was the confiscated property of a fugitive from justice and thereby belonged to the sheriff of the county. I had the pleasure of paying my own expenses in the chase.

Six months later I was in Utah buying cattle and was informed of the next escapade of Butch and his partner. The Castle Gate Coal Company, located at Castle Gate, Utah, was a big producer and employed many men. The boys had established a camp a few miles below. They dressed up in blue denim pants and jumpers and riding two old mares bareback, they applied to the superintendent for work. They were informed there were no openings at present, but to hang around for a few days when they would probably have vacancies. They called at the office each morning for three days — that was pay day, and as the paymaster stepped off the train, a gun was pressed against his side and he was relieved of his bag containing the pay-roll.

A clerk in the office, a hundred feet away, saw the holdup and walked out on a porch with a Winchester. He was covered by Butch, whose rapid-fire talk induced him to drop his gun. They mounted their horses and raced to their camp where two speedy, grain-fed, steel-shod horses, all saddled and ready, were awaiting them. In the pay-roll bag were 900 silver dollars — these they threw aside — too much weight for speed. This they could afford to leave, as $14,000 in currency remained. They were soon on their way to their hide-away, near the head of the Virgin River. They stopped long enough to tell a road crew that the Castle Gate Coal Company had been robbed and to tell the sheriff that they would have the robbers by the time they caught up.

Their hideout was called "The Hole in the Wall," a freak of nature; a faulting of the red sandstone had left a level of four hundred feet square, partly roofed by sandstone, a natural fence, fifteen feet high, enclosed it and the only entrance was through a hole in the wall just wide enough for a saddle or pack horse to enter. This rendezvous they had stocked with hay, grain and provisions. A cold spring flowed from the upper end. They closed the opening with a heavy steel gate anchored deep in the rock — always locked.

Then followed the hold-up of mercantile houses and finally three robberies of express and mail cars. An express detective informed me that as it was impossible to arrest them, negotiations had concluded a truce by which for a consideration they were to go to Honduras, never to return. There they bought a herd and for years raised cattle. An American engineer in Honduras informed me that the old bandit instinct finally came to the fore. They learned that a very rich gold mine was packing out gold bullion by mule train. The boys captured the train, but two hundred pounds of bullion on each mule made a quick get-away difficult. They were soon captured by Honduras cavalry and immediately executed. It is a safe bet that Butch Cassidy faced the firing squad with a smile.

BOOK FOUR:
A Mysterious Death in Gypsum Valley

1: A Veteran Homestead

❦ After the end of World War I, with the Veterans returning home after making the world safe for democracy, there were thousands who had left home as youths and returned as men who were ready to go out in the world and make their mark. Most of these did not have a job before they entered the service, being just fresh out of high school, and therefore did not have a job to come home to. Also they were not trained in any field of employment. They knew how to use a weapon and obey orders. That is about the extent of what had been learned during their stay in the army. They were not the same little boys who had lived at home with Momma and Papa and most did not care to return to the old home as a permanent thing. But those who were farm-raised still had the love of the land and the yearning to get back to it. They were ready to go out on their own.

The government provided a small monthly payment for these men, and for any of them who wanted to go west where there was lots of available land, their service record gave them a certain amount of preference over non-veterans when it came to filing for a homestead. The homestead requirement was something like: build a cabin of at least ten feet by ten feet, fence the land and live there for five years and it was yours. There were certain land claims that required a person to irrigate, if the water was available, at least twenty acres of his claim.

2: Gypsum Valley

❦ One young Veteran of that terrible war, who shall remain anonymous, came west in search of land to homestead. His travels eventually brought him to the western part of San Miguel County, Colorado, in an area known as "Gypsum Valley." Here, lots of land was available and with the aid of maps and surveys, he located one hundred and forty acres that was to meet his dream of owning a piece of this world. He set about getting the necessary materials for his cabin and in a short time had a livable structure on the land. About then he decided that he would need to have some farm animals to contribute to his ability to survive. There would have to be a milk cow, chickens, a pig or two and a saddle horse. The horse would be his mode of transportation where ever he needed to go. These animals would have to have shelter and confinement so the proud land owner began digging back into a hillside until he had a room large enough to contain them. He then covered it over with poles and sod for a roof. The horse would have to do with the shelter of a cedar tree until more room could be made in the hillside.

After a few visits with other homesteaders in the area about the possibilities of dry farming, Mr. Anonymous decided to get enough machinery to break up some of his land and plant a crop of wheat or oats. There were many successful dry farms in western San Miguel County and his could also be one. He got another horse so as to have a team to pull the plow and seeder and began his first experience in dry land farming.

For some unknown reason this homesteader, in just a few years, was making plans to dispose of his property. This advertisement appeared in a well-circulated newspaper: For Sale: One Hundred Forty Acre Dry Farm. Some machinery and farm animals. Located in western San Miguel County in "Gypsum Valley."

3: Campbell's Dream

In another part of Colorado lived a young man, Ivan Campbell, who, as he put it, was sick and tired of irrigating on his grandfather's ranch on Salt Creek about three miles east of Collbran, Colorado. It was daylight-to-dark every summer day just following that darn water all over the ranch. He was ready for a change and he spotted that ad about the dry farm and suddenly became interested. It would be great to have a farm with no irrigating. He took the newspaper over to his brother-in-law, Asa Merrick, and asked him what he thought of the idea of going to look at it with the probability of buying it. Merrick was well situated on a small farm himself and raising a son who at this time was five years old.

Wanting to do something for the brother of his wife Ethel, Merrick said that if Campbell wanted to make the trip he would go along. As soon as the plans to go became a family discussion, five-year-old Ray Merrick wanted to go along too. His dad tried to tell him that it would be a long hard trip even for the adults, but the child's intense enthusiasm about going and his many promises to be good and not get in the way and help with all the camp chores, won his dad over into allowing the child to go along. Young Ray was wild with excitement and almost running in circles getting his personal things together for the trip. He would have many chances to regret that he ever wanted to go on that trip, but such are childish whims. The adults made up their bedrolls and fashioned a chuck box for grub and utensils and with a suitcase or two they were ready to load it all on the train and proceed to the point where they would have to leave the railroad and begin the last part of the trip with a team and wagon.

The train trip was pure excitement for young Ray. The old "Galloping Goose" was a thrill to ride anyway and the high trestles and sharp curves hanging along the canyon walls had him totally absorbed. The train-ride time passed quickly and they were soon pulling into the depot at Placerville. Campbell and Merrick unloaded all their stuff on the depot platform and went to the local livery to rent a team and wagon. At the same time they purchased several bales of hay and about fifty pounds of oats for the horses. They also procured a water barrel just in case the trip should turn out to be through a lot of dry country. With all their camp outfit loaded in the wagon, they were ready to start on their way to investigate this dry farm possibility.

The route they were to follow was down the San Miguel River road for twelve twisting, torturous miles. The road at that time had to go up and over all of the ridges that ran down from the top of the canyon side and ended in huge vertical cliffs at the water's edge and it made for very tough traveling, especially for the loaded freight wagons that were on the road every day from Placerville and Paradox, loaded both ways. One such bad hill on this river road was called "Commissioner Hill" and it got that name because it took the County Commissioners a full six months of arguing over which was the most feasible route for the money to build the grade necessary to go over the hill and down the other side or to blast a road around the base of the cliff. Finally, they decided that to go over the top was the least costly and that is the way it was built.

One of the several "Galloping Goose" units that carried mail and passengers on the Rio Grande Southern Railroad.

Photo by Author

That one hill on the route caused more teamster profanity, more breakdowns of harness and wagon and more lost time than any other part of the trip. Because of this hill, the freighters had to travel in pairs so that when they came to Commissioner Hill the teamster in the rear could unhook one team and with a chain go to the front of the lead wagon and hook onto it. With the extra horsepower they could get up and over the top. Then the wagon was blocked from rolling and both teams were unhooked and taken back to the rear and the process repeated. When the top of the hill was reached, the proper teams were hitched to the proper wagons and the teamsters traveled on until the next hill was reached. Not all of them required extra teams to get over but there were quite a few that did.

For the two men and the boy, this was all negotiated in fairly good time as the wagon was not loaded heavily and the team was well rested and wanting to go. Soon they reached the bridge over the river and began another two and a half miles of steep, narrow grade with very few turn outs until they had reached the top of "Norwood Hill." Now the traveling was easy with it being nearly all down hill and just at dusk the trio pulled into the freight station stopover called Coventry where there was a livery and a hotel. They were able to get accommodations for themselves in the hotel and the horses were cared for in the livery along with numerous teams of the freighters.

The supper bell was clanging by the time all was done for the horses and everyone assembled in the dining room to be served a family-style meal. As everyone there put in long hard days, not much time was lost between the evening meal and getting into bed and almost before they realized that they had been asleep the same bell that had called them in for supper was clanging again for breakfast. All hands rolled out of bed and the breakfast was soon over with.

The three travelers harnessed their team and hitched up to the wagon. They had gotten some precise directions from the hotel manager as to finding the road they had to turn off on when they reached the little community of Redvale. They were soon on their way. Redvale was another stopover on the freight route. Sometimes when the roads were a bottomless mud hole, five miles a day was all the teams could make. Merrick was handling the reins of the team and they were soon at the turn-off point where the road went south and crossed Naturita Canyon on a road much like the one up Norwood Hill.

From there on it was due south several miles until the road they were on joined with one going to the west and that was the one that would take them into the area known as Dry Creek Basin. Several miles of traveling due west and they arrived at a sharp turn to the south. This place had the name of Beard's Corner and it got that name from a settler there who went into the town of Naturita looking for his wife. He found her in a place where he didn't like finding her and was so enraged that he killed her right there and then hauled her body out into Dry Creek Basin and buried her at the location of the turn that still bears his name.

After rounding the curve the party continued on south and it seemed to them that the road was skirting around the eastern end of a high ridge called "The Gyp Rim" which was soon behind them. Looming up ahead of them was a mountain which they knew was where Gypsum Valley began and ran northwesterly for some twenty miles. The place they were looking for was in the "Head Of Gyp" and in just another mile or so and they were going down a small ridge that was known as the separation between Dry Creek Basin and the Head of Gyp. They were almost there and it was getting late evening. The first wagon track turning to the south in the Head Of Gyp would take them directly to the homestead cabin. Neither of the adults riding in that wagon had any inclination about what was waiting for them when they pulled into the space between the cabin and the corral where the milk cow was.

4: Something Terribly Wrong

It took only one look to realize that things weren't quite right as the cow was down on her side and seemingly in very bad shape if not dead. Two head of horses part-way up on a hillside with drooping heads and gaunt, shrunken bellies were what next met the bewildered gaze of the visitors. Then a pitiful looking, half-starved dog, snarling and snapping and foaming at the mouth came out from behind the cabin. There was a terribly depressed atmosphere all about the place. Before alighting from the wagon Asa Merrick turned to his brother-in-law and spoke. "There is something terribly wrong here," he said and Campbell promptly agreed.

They told five-year-old Ray to stay in the wagon while they investigated. They dismounted from their seat on the wagon and approached the cabin. The dog stood menacingly before them and would not let them any closer and refused any friendly advances the pair tried to make. At about that time the men noticed a foul and sickening odor coming from the cabin. They knew immediately what was wrong. The owner was dead in the cabin and probably had been for a week. The cow was nearly dead for want of water and the horses were as bad off but because they were out loose had very likely been able to get some moisture from the dew on the grass in the early mornings.

The men needed to get to the cabin and know the truth. The dog was still a problem and would not let them any closer. Campbell walked down to the barn and found a pitchfork and with that as a weapon was able to make the dog give ground and they made their way up to the door. As soon as they opened the door they were immediately sick from the smell and the sight of a badly swollen man's body, in the early stages of decomposition, but still seated at the table. His upper body was folded over to rest on the table. The lower part still in the chair. It was a strange way for a dead person to be found. Parts of a .45 Colt pistol were laying about on the table as though the owner had been cleaning it or possibly repairing it. Death must have been instantaneous, as if from a massive heart attack. Hanging from a couple of pegs on the ridgepole of the cabin was an excellent, nearly new rifle, fully loaded. Scattered about on the table were numerous unsigned checks and some other personal things including a purse containing seventeen dollars and one gold coin.

Outside the cabin were several water barrels that were over half full. Apparently the one who was living there had to haul his water from a spring or creek somewhere up in the Dry Creek Basin area. There was no live water anywhere in the Head Of Gyp. Campbell took a bucket of water down to the corral but the cow was so far gone she couldn't raise her head. One of the horses came down from the hill and warily approached the bucket. Campbell thought surely he would drink but the horse was crazed from thirst and at the first smell of the water he took off back to the hillside and in company of the other horse disappeared over the hill into the timber.

Merrick brought the rifle from the cabin and with a well placed bullet between the eyes, he put the suffering cow to rest. The dog was acting so strangely and with such a mean attitude the men feared that, after his master had died, he had gone out hunting for his food and contracted rabies. He wasn't to be trusted and with the small boy there it was too much of a risk to have him around. Another well-placed bullet and the dog was no longer a problem. What else were they to do with these starved out animals in their terrible condition? To leave them in their misery would have been just as cruel. In a case of this kind a bullet is swift and merciful. The fate of the horses was never known. Just over the mountain to the south of where they were last seen was a large area inhabited by a band of wild horses. Perhaps with the inborn instinct to seek their own kind and herd up they may have gotten wind of them and joined that bunch of wild horses.

5: A Proper Burial

Night was descending rapidly on this trio who had came to this place to investigate the for sale ad and see for themselves if they wanted to buy a dry farm. They had found death instead and the whole picture had now taken on a very undesirable aspect. The boy, Ray, was tired and hungry, and so were the two men. They were not about to use the cabin for any reason so a small fire was built out in the yard and coffee was soon brewing. After a quick supper of sardines and pork and beans, washed down with scalding hot coffee, the men started looking for a place to lay their bedrolls. Poor little Ray, having never been around any deaths, was quite depressed about the dead man and also about the dog and cow. It had all been sort of dumped on him all at once. The coyotes were beginning to yelp and cry from the hilltop where the horses disappeared and there seemed to be quite a few which made it seem like they were much closer. The smell of death was everywhere and probably would attract more than just coyotes. Where were the men going to sleep? Where was a safe place for little Ray and the men?

It was near dark now and they had to decide quickly. They decided that on the sod roof of the barn was probably the best place so they drove the team and wagon over near there and turned the horses loose in the corral with feed and water. Their bedrolls were soon laid out flat and the trio began preparing for bed. Merrick was in possession of the rifle but he turned it over to Campbell as he seemed to be a lot more concerned about the howling coyotes. They set up such a chorus of yips and cries that sleep was impossible for all but little Ray. He was so "sacked out" that hardly anything could have awakened him.

The coyotes came closer later in the night and Campbell fired a shot in the general direction of where they were. It didn't seem to bother them any. They howled and carried on just as bad. Every so often Campbell would send another bullet up that way more as a defensive measure than anything. Later in the night the coyotes let up a little in their yips and cries and the two men thought they might get some sleep. Just as they were about to doze off they heard some heavy footfalls of an animal that had come down around the corral. Whatever it was, it didn't bother the team any. If it had been one of the loose horses there should have been some low nickers and snorts of recognition passed between them. Campbell fired another shot up towards the coyotes and hoped for a little silence and a little sleep. Daylight came before he had either of them.

During the night of sleeplessness, Merrick and Campbell decided that come morning, they had best bury the man in the cabin. It would take a full day, all told, for them to get to a telephone and call authorities and for them to arrive down there. The body would be in terrible shape by then. To get him into the ground and properly covered seemed like the right and Christian thing to do. After they had some breakfast they took a look around for a burial place. Something that had gone unnoticed was an outdoor privy that the inhabitant had built for personal use and comfort. He had started digging a hole to move it over which was about two feet wide, four feet long and about four feet deep.

Campbell wondered aloud to Merrick that it might have been the digging that brought on the demise of the resident. If that were true the man had literally "dug his own grave." Campbell and Merrick just widened and lengthened the hole for a suitable grave. The fellow had a canvas bed tarp in the cabin so Campbell laid it out flat on the cabin floor and they laid the body out on it as straight as they could. They placed the gold coin on his chest and rolled the canvas about him and used the bed rope to wrap the bundle up in a tight roll. Then they carried it out to the grave and laid the stranger to rest.

Five-year-old Ray Merrick watched all this procedure with a great amount of wondering and awe. It was something that very few five-year-olds are permitted to see. The covering of the grave was done in good time and before the men left the site they hitched the team to the wagon and drove down below the corral where they had spotted a section of an old spike tooth harrow. They hooked this behind the wagon with a chain and dragged it over the grave and parked it there. This was done with the idea in mind that predators would not be able to dig into the grave. The rifle was returned to the place it had occupied in the cabin and everything was left exactly as it had been found, minus one corpse. It was almost noon before the trio pulled out of there for the return trip to Coventry where they would spend the night. Upon arriving there, Merrick called the sheriff of San Miguel County and reported to him in exact detail the full scope of events that had taken place since they had pulled into the homestead of the dead man.

The sheriff didn't seem greatly impressed by the events that had transpired. He praised Merrick and Campbell for doing the right thing. Apparently they saved the county a lot of trouble and expense, because there is no record of a sheriff, deputy sheriff or coroner that ever made a trip down there to investigate. I have searched the records thoroughly and it just isn't there. So far I have been unsuccessful in finding anything that was put in the newspaper about an unattended death in Gypsum Valley.

The information that I have written in this account was given to me in 1993 by Ray Merrick who at the time was seventy-seven-years old and was still alive and in good health. He lives in Aurora, Colorado. He had asked questions of his father and uncle many times and was told this story on those occasions. Later on in his life, Ray Merrick enlisted in the Civilian Conservation Corps and was stationed at a Camp (D-G-11-C) located at Indian Springs in Dry Creek Basin. He spent a couple of years there and was part of the work crews that built many lasting improvements in western San Miguel County.

BOOK FIVE:

A Cancer in His Gut — Honey Dunham's Revenge

1: Honey

❧ Three men's lives were crossed by a star, a star that brought death, drunkenness or disgrace to them all. It all began in Disappointment Valley where two of the three grew up as friends and playmates. They married sisters and many a wagging tongue spread the thoughts they had each chosen wrong. As the years rolled by the same busy gossips could plainly see that the romance had faded from the lives of the two couples. One half of the pairs was plainly more interested in the other's half than his own. Jim Nash and Lena Dunham were being seen together more and more. They rode the range together as one, and many were the romantic nights spent in some out-of-the-way cow camp. The valley's tongues were busy. There would be a shootin' and a buryin' before it was ended.

John Dunham, known as Jack and also Johnnie, didn't have much control over his wife. She was very set in her ways, disliked house work and family chores and only seemed to care for the things that really pleased her, such as riding after the cattle in the company of Jim Nash. Jack Dunham could see it all coming to a head and tried to teach his eleven-year-old son, Irving, to accept the inevitable fact that his mother Lena wouldn't be with them much longer. Jack and Lena were destined to part but not in the way it came about.

Lena did care a lot about her son. She doted over him much like an old hen with one chick. She had called him "Honey" for so long that a lot of other people had picked up on it until he was much better known as Honey Dunham than by his given name of Irving. Even at eleven years of age he was developing a hatred for Jim Nash that would last his entire lifetime and only get worse with age. His reasons were soon to increase.

2: A Killing

¶ The news spread up and down the valley as fast as a good saddle horse and rider could spread the word. Jim Nash and Jack Dunham had met and argued over Lena. Shots were fired and Jack Dunham fell mortally wounded. The Nash version of the shooting stated that Jim Nash and his son Earl were driving cattle up the valley past the ranch of Johnnie Dunham. Jack (Johnnie) was out in the yard chopping wood and had a placed a pistol within easy reach should he need it for some reason. He hailed the Nash cowboys and Jim rode up to the yard, rifle in hand. There was a bitter exchange of words about Jim's attention to Lena. Words led to accusations and then to threats and Jack Dunham made a grab for his pistol on the nearby stump. Jim Nash shot and killed him before he could fire a shot.

Lena, in her version of the shooting, said her husband was in the shop doing some blacksmithing when the cattle herd went by. She said that Jack got his pistol and hollered at Jim Nash from the doorway of the shop. Jim drew his Winchester from the saddle boot and dismounted. In the exchange of shots Jack Dunham fell with a death wound. John Dunham was an intelligent man, a good cattleman, farmer and hard worker. He didn't have a stupid bone in his body. If Lena's story was true and Jack deliberately went up against a rifle with a pistol at long range — well, that was stupidity and suicide. Some people thought that Lena shot her husband from behind while he was engaged in exchanging shots with Jim Nash. Jim took the blame for the killing because he figured he could beat the case on a plea of self-defense.

The story that was told to me by Fred Sharp, who was one of the world's greatest story tellers, and for whom I have the greatest respect, goes like this: Jack Dunham was in bed with pneumonia and sick enough to die. Jim Nash had come to the Dunham home and he and Lena were out in the shop, behaving outrageously. Jack got up from his sick bed and with pistol in hand went to the outbuilding to have it out with Jim Nash. His son Irving was with him. As he stepped through the door of the shop, from behind the door, Jim Nash placed a pistol to the back of his head and fired. Honey Dunham always said that he saw Nash kill his dad. Jack Dunham fell dead right at the feet of his son. Honey Dunham swore an oath of vengeance that someday he would kill Jim Nash. Of the three versions of the killing two things seem to be consistent. Lena was present at the scene and Jack Dunham was shot from behind.

3: *A New Marriage*

After the "shootin' and the buryin' " was over Jim's wife Tennie moved out of the Nash home and settled into a house in another part of the valley. Jim had successfully beat the charge of murder as the jury was undecided and the judge dismissed the case. Two years after the death of Jack Dunham, Lena and Jim Nash were married. Her two children, May and Irving, went to live with her and Jim. As a step-father, Jim tried to be good to the children of the man he had killed. May accepted him and didn't hold any bad feelings. Honey was just the opposite. He wouldn't listen to any advice or suggestions. He hated Jim and did everything he could to make his life difficult. Jim and Lena gave him land and cattle and a good start in life.

Revenge was such a cancer in his guts that Honey never tried to make a good life for himself. He took to drinking and carousing and spending money recklessly until he had lost all that had been given to him. His folks gave him another start. This time he found a wife and settled down for a few years. They had three sons and it looked like Honey Dunham might be on the right track for a change. Soon the old life of drunkenness and irresponsibility took control. He repeatedly wrote checks for his booze that weren't worth the paper they were written on. His mother steadfastly refused to give up on him and made good on the checks until she and Jim were nearly broke. She finally had to quit coming to his rescue and he had to do a short stay in the penitentiary for his shortcomings. This was the end of his marriage and family. It did nothing for Honey except give him time to sit and brood and plan how some day he would kill Jim Nash.

Remarkable as it may seem Honey Dunham still had a few friends and sympathizers. People would take him in for a few days, sober him up, give him a few dollars and send him on his way. The first place he could buy a jug of wine would be his first stop and from then on it was just going from friend to friend until he had lost them all. Honey Dunham was constantly in trouble because of his seemingly incurable trait of wanting to cheat while playing cards. It didn't matter what kind of a game it was, he just had to cheat. He couldn't play any other way.

4: A Card Fight

After a week of drunken partying and finally getting jailed to sober up, Honey Dunham was in a sorry state. His step-father decided to try to do one last thing for him. He would take him along to the winter range cow camp of Fritz Johannison on Montezuma Creek just across the Utah state line. There would be no booze of any kind and perhaps Honey could get sobered up and be of some use to the world. He did get sober but it only made his thoughts clearer and brought back the millions of times he vowed he would kill Jim Nash. During this time in the 1920s a .38 Colt automatic pistol was fast becoming the most popular sidearm and was usually carried in an abdominal holster. Honey Dunham had one and was well schooled on how to use it.

Jim Nash and Irving Dunham being thrown together in a wilderness cabin was a volatile situation and very likely to explode on short notice. It was evening, April 13, 1922. Four people were seated at a card table. Two of them were involved in a game of poker. As usual Honey Dunham was cheating and was caught in the act by Jim Nash. Nash called him some pretty dirty names, told him he "hated his guts" and suggested he get out of the country before he cut his "damned head off." At this point Nash reached for his pocket knife and started for Dunham.

Honey Dunham was well prepared for just such a situation. He had been over it in his mind thousands of times. He knew someday he would kill Jim Nash and had done it in his mind over and over again. It was all so simple. Just draw the pistol and empty it into the body of the charging Nash. Four bullets were closely grouped in the chest cavity and one had shattered the outstretched hand before entering the shoulder as Jim Nash raised his hand in defense when he saw what was taking place and felt the bullets ripping through his lungs. He was dead when he hit the floor. Honey Dunham had finally done it, after seventeen years of planning and waiting. Now it was done. The cancer in his guts could finally quiet down. He had revenge.

5: *Self Defense*

Honey Dunham went to Monticello, Utah, and turned himself in to the sheriff. After testimony by Rexford Perkins and Fritz Johannison a charge of murder was placed on Dunham. He was released on bond and one year later was brought to trial. His lawyer successfully pleaded his case to the jury. The basis of the defense was that Jim Nash was known to be a dangerous man, having killed Dunham's father seventeen years previous, and that he had threatened the life of Honey Dunham and was in the act of taking out his knife to "cut his damned head off." The defense claimed that Irving Dunham had the right to defend himself. The jury believed it and Honey Dunham was acquitted of all charges. He died in 1963 at the age of sixty-four.

BOOK SIX:
Murder Along the Fenceline

Tuesday, June 17, 1924, didn't appear to be any different to Fred Dobler and Cliff Davis than any other day. They were busily engaged in building a fence separating a Forest Service parcel of lease land from a forty-acre tract, known as the Jim Skinner place, that Fred Dobler of the Nucla Sheep, Land & Cattle Co. had sold to one John Wood, a rancher in the Sanborn Park area. The fence had been ordered by the law firm of Catlin & Catlin who had foreclosed on the land because of non-payment of the $2000 promissory note given them by John Wood.

Several days fence work had already been completed when Wood came by and noticed what was going on. He claimed that he had not been served any notice by the law firm about the foreclosure. To him it appeared that two men were putting up a fence that he didn't want and one that would only be harmful to his operation. The best water and grass for his livestock were on the land that would be closed off by the fence. He asked the men to stop the work on the fence. He said he would be by in a couple of days to check on it.

Instead of sitting at home and brooding over the unwanted fence, Wood should have been in Montrose conferring with his banker and the attorneys who closed him out on the property. He might have had an entirely different attitude. But he didn't, and good on his word, he was there two days later and was carrying a rifle. Davis and Dobler were not armed and had no reason to carry firearms out on the job. John Wood was an unsavory character, not well liked, and feared by most of the ranchers of the area. He had never seriously harmed anyone but his threats involving guns and how he might use them kept most of the people a little edgy when he was around. He had a bulldozing attitude. He never spoke of his past or where he had come from. People suspected that he had another life and wanted it kept secret.

Wood appeared out of the brush not more than sixty or seventy feet from the fence builders, rifle in hand. He asked Dobler why he was still putting up the fence. Dobler replied that he had the forest land leased. Wood asked, "What did you do with the note that I gave for the property?" Dobler said that he had nothing to do with that. Wood then ordered them to start tearing out the fence immediately and he would give them ten minutes to get it done. Dobler said he would start taking out the fence when Catlin ordered it done. Wood again said, "You've got ten minutes." They both pleaded with him. Ten minutes wasn't nearly enough time. It would take all day to tear down what they had constructed so far. Wood was adamant as to the allotted time and pulled out his watch, loaded his rifle and called out "Ten minutes is all you've got!" The men were trying to get the fence down but they had done a good job of constructing it and it didn't come down easily. Time was ticking away and John Wood watched every minute of it disappear from the face of the watch.

When ten minutes was up he opened fire on the two men with his .303 Savage rifle. The first bullet ripped through the flesh of the upper arm of Fred Dobler tearing away most of the arm. The men pleaded with Wood not to shoot again. Their pleas fell upon deaf ears. Wood yelled out, "Your time's up." Another shot pierced Dobler's abdomen and the soft nosed hunting bullet did massive destruction to the entire stomach and abdomen. It is hard to believe what a high velocity, mushrooming bullet can do to soft tissue. The two men begged for mercy and for Wood not to shoot any more. Dobler said, "Don't shoot me again John, you've got me." He didn't shoot again. He just mounted his horse and rode away as if nothing had happened and he had other business somewhere else. As John Wood rode out of sight Dobler spoke to Cliff Davis. "I hope I have friends enough to get him. He is insane!"

Cliff Davis made Dobler as comfortable as possible and went for help. Dobler was in terrible pain and shock and begged not to be left alone. Davis had to go for help. There were telephones in the Sanborn Park area and a quick call was made to the Norwood doctor to advise him that they were going to try and bring Dobler to Norwood, about twenty miles away. Charley Irvine was contacted about the use of his car, which he gladly offered, and Fred was loaded into it to start the trip. In only a few miles it was apparent that Dobler could never stand the slow and punishing ride. His pain was too great. They returned to the Irvine ranch and called the Norwood doctor again and advised him of the situation. Dr. Blair started immediately for the home of the Irvines. John Wood rode to the sawmill and told the people there what had happened. He claimed self-defense. He got a packhorse from the pasture. He made up a pack outfit suitable for an extensive trip and everyone there thought he was headed for the Blue Mountains of Utah which was an outlaw hangout along the Outlaw Trail. There he would be safe from the law as very few sheriffs dared to enter the outlaws' domain. At Charley Irvine's ranch he had a change of heart and unloaded the packhorse leaving it and the camp outfit there. He mounted his horse and started the fifty-mile ride to Montrose to turn himself in to the sheriff. He knew he had killed a man and would have to face the penalty. He stopped awhile in the pinyons a few miles out of Montrose and awaited the coming of daylight. He would then finish the trip.

About the time John Wood was making his camp on the outskirts of Montrose, Fred Dobler finally succumbed to the terrible wounds he had received. After an unbelievable amount of suffering and pain, death was a blessing to the tortured man. Upon arriving in Montrose Wood went to a cafe and ordered breakfast and wrote a check to pay for the meal. He then proceeded to the sheriff's office and told his story. Another version of the story states that Wood used the telephone in the No Delay Cafe and called the sheriff who came and arrested John there. By whatever means he was in custody of the sheriff. At first he claimed self-defense saying that he thought Dobler was armed and was reaching for a gun when he opened fire. This story was blasted to pieces by witnesses from Sanborn Park when they arrived in Montrose.

When Wood was arraigned before the district judge and asked how he pleaded, he said, "Your honor, I am guilty to some of the charge but I am not guilty to the rest of it." His attorney, Dan Hughes of Montrose, advised him to plead guilty to the charges as they were read. This he did. This was an unusual day for the court. Two murderers were brought up before the Judge to hear their pleas and to set dates for trial. The other one was a Mexican who shot and killed a fellow onion-field worker over personal differences. Both were unprovoked, cold-blooded killings.

When John Wood's self-defense story was blasted to pieces the only reason he had for shooting Fred Dobler was, " He shouldn't have argued with me. I got mad and lost my temper and after the first shot was fired I don't remember anything that happened." Dr. Fred Schermerhorn, the coroner, said of the slaying of Dobler: "It was the most brutal, cold-blooded, senseless killing that I have ever been called to investigate." John Wood was tried before District Judge Straud M. Logan on the charge of second-degree murder. First-degree murder was not available as Wood had not planned on killing anyone before the arguments developed. His carrying of the rifle was just more of the attitude that made people fear him. His attitude that fatal morning could have been worsened by a severe "bawling out" he had received from one of the women at the sawmill. It was reported that she had called him everything but a gentleman over what she called "the stealing of her saddle." He had left there in low spirits with his head hanging down. The jury was not out very long and returned with the verdict of "guilty as charged." He was sentenced to life in the penitentiary.

This story has interested me for a long time. I was born in Placerville, Colorado, on May 31, 1924, in a house that was known as the Dobler Place.

BOOK SEVEN:
A Day in the Life of a Cowboy

Jack Bailey, a cowboy-cattleman, sat alone in the cabin at the Circle Cross summer camp. He had made plans to start moving his cattle to a pasture near Nucla, Colorado where he had bought the haystacks that had been produced that summer. That would be his winter quarters. Several days had been spent gathering the cattle from the big pasture on the Circle Cross range and putting them into a smaller unit where he had irrigated the land and saved the grass for just this very occasion. It would only hold the livestock for a specified number of days. He had sent word by the mail carrier to two of his friends who were expected to be there on the morning he was to start out with the cattle. Otherwise he would have to go it alone and would have to hope for a lot of good luck during the three day trip.

The evening before the scheduled start of the cattle drive several rowdy young cowboys, out on a drinking spree, drove up to the cabin. They wanted to have a few drinks with Jack before continuing their journey over to the bootlegger's domain, known as Disappointment Valley, to replenish their dwindling supply of whiskey. Their intentions were good. Just a friendly and neighborly act done by most of the cowboys. The timing for the visit was terrible. Jack was to have the cattle on the trail and moving by sun-up. The cowboys stayed until after midnight and everyone drank more than they should have.

Jack awakened at daylight, fed his horses and fixed himself some breakfast. He had a bear of a hangover and couldn't eat a bite. His cowdog was the recipient of the meal and Jack made ready to leave the cabin for the winter. There was no sign of the help that he had sent for. It was beginning to snow very hard and worse, the snow was driven by a stiff wind; but Jack was committed to start the drive. There was no more feed in the holding pasture and over a foot of snow covered the ground out in the big pasture. Turning the cattle back into it was definitely out of the question.

Before leaving the cabin Jack stuffed a nearly empty whiskey bottle into his saddle bag. Thinking that later in the day a drink or two might make him feel better. He certainly couldn't feel much worse. There is that old cow country saying which is supposed to make you feel better: "a little hair off the dog that bit you," but it is small consolation when you feel really bad. He was riding his faithful cowhorse "Johnny".

Johnny was named for John Daniels who caught him from a wild bunch of horses, broke him to ride, and traded him to Jack Bailey. Jack was leading a packhorse with his bedroll and supplies. The extra horse was turned loose to follow along behind the cattle. He just happened to be the coal black horse everyone called "Ole Nigger." He had bucked off every cowboy in that whole country that had tried to ride him. His one forgiving trait was that when he wanted to be well-mannered he was the best cowhorse you could ask for and he loved to drive cattle. And he would do it alone. Any cow critter that strayed off the trail would have that black horse right after her, ears laid back and teeth nipping at her hocks. With such a horse and the cowdog Jack felt he could make the drive. If the cowboys should arrive at the cabin they could trail the cattle and catch up later in the day. Now that it was snowing so hard Jack didn't expect to see them or anyone else.

Jack Bailey was an early day cowboy in the southwest. He is shown here at age ninety.

Courtesy of Jack Bailey

The snow continued to fall and at times it fell so hard that only the cattle directly in front of his horse were visible. If the cattle hadn't known the trail, having traveled it for years, they could never have known where they were going. Along about noon Jack felt the pangs of hunger nagging at his innards. He hadn't carried anything with him to eat because eating was the last thing he figured he could do that day. But the hunger wouldn't go away, so he began to look through the bunch for his milk cow. Jack always kept one at his summer camp so he could have butter and cream. He soon spotted her through the falling snow and cut her out from the bunch. He drove her off a short distance from the herd, near a pine tree, and roped her and tied her to the tree. Jack emptied out the whiskey bottle and milked into it until it was nearly full. He turned the faithful cow loose, capped the bottle and mounted his horse. The warm milk in his belly made him feel much better and he drank from it all afternoon. How's that for a warm meal on the trail and not even stopping to cook.

Late in the afternoon the snow started letting up a little. The cattle were nearing the vicinity of Redvale, Colorado. Awhile later, as the snowfall continued to lessen, Jack could see down the road about a mile. To his great surprise there was a team of horses pulling a hayrack loaded with about a ton of loose hay. Driving them was Miles Naff a cattleman of the Redvale-Shenandoah area. How he ever knew that Jack was on the trail with his cattle, and would need feed for them and his horses that night, will probably never be known. Call it insight, cattleman savvy or what you may.

Nevertheless Jack was very pleased and surprised. They fed the hay to the cattle and Jack turned his horses loose to eat with them. He then seated himself on the hayrack, having accepted the invitation that Miles Naff extended for him to have supper and stay all night. That wasn't all of the story. Mr. Naff spent the next two days helping Jack drive the cattle to their winter destination. It was typical of the friendliness and brotherhood of the cowboy fraternity in those good old days of the wild West.

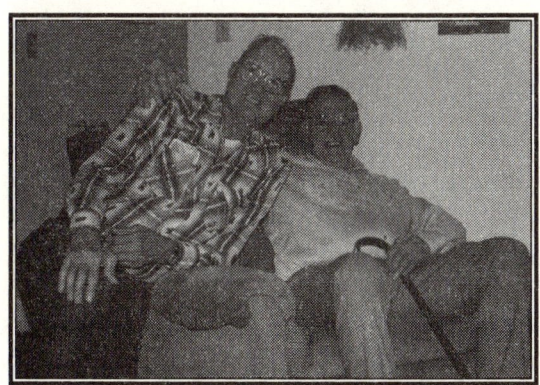

The author (left) and his friend, Jack Bailey, at age 91 at Cheyenne, Wyoming in 1993.
Photo by Author

¶ Howard Greager was born in Placerville, Colorado on May 31, 1924. His mother was of a pioneer Delta County family and his father was a New Hampshire native who had to move west because he could no longer live in the damp New England climate. He had been afflicted with asthma since early childhood and needed a high, dry climate to survive. He learned to be a cowboy and that was his chosen profession until a growing

The four Greager children and cousin are all on one horse at Beaver Mesa Ranch in 1926. Author is at the front.
Greager Family Photo

family demanded more of his time and a much greater income. For many years he was a saloon keeper in Placerville and saw the best of the boom years when Placerville was the largest shipping point for cattle anywhere in the United States. He later turned to ranching and son Howard spent his earliest years there.

Betty and Howard Greager celebrate fifty years of marriage on October 1, 1999.
Greager Family Photo

Howard grew up with a horse between his legs. Even when only a few months old his mother would place him on a pillow in front of the saddle on a nice gentle old mare so she could ride over to the neighbors for an afternoon visit. By the time he was two years old there would be five brothers and sisters riding bareback on one horse. The kids took lots of falls and were regularly scraped off by low hanging branches. People said cowboys did not mind getting bucked off or taking a fall and to them it was part of growing up. Being raised among ranching families had its advantages.

Howard spent many years as a cowboy working on ranches in Colorado, Utah and Arizona. Like his father he had to seek better paying work when he married Betty fifty years ago on October 1, 1949 and their family of two boys and a girl arrived. He started writing short stories for a newspaper in 1965 and then compiled those works and more for his first book published in 1990. Since then he has put four more books on the market. All are true western history.

This mountain cabin was the home of the author for the first six years of his life
Greager Family Photo

All that is left of the author's childhood home after being neglected and uninhabited for seventy years.
Greager Family Photo

Expanded Bibliography

W. J. (Bill) Bentenson is a distant relative of Butch Cassidy who has a tremendous interest in the activities of his great uncle while he lived and worked in southwestern Colorado. You are warmly thanked for your contribution to this book.

The book, *Monticello Journal* by authors George and Faye Muhlestein was very useful. Thanks to them for their kind permission to use necessary history from Monticello, Utah. I made good use of the book *Where Eagles Winter* by Wilma C. Bankston. Many thanks to her for permission to use the necessary material in researching this book.

A special thanks to Tom Bradford of Blanding, Utah for his great care in photographing the winter hideout of the outlaw Tom McCarty. Eileen Brown, daughter of former Sheriff of San Miguel County Guy Warrick. Thank you so much for your photo contribution. To the Cortez Public Library goes a special thanks for access and help with the files and tapes during the research for this book.

To *The Denver Post* goes thanks for contributing copies from the 1941 newspapers that were needed for research. To the *Dolores Star* goes my gratitude for reprints from the 1938 newspaper, which was greatly appreciated and contributed significantly to the completion of this book.

The LDS Church Historical Society of Salt Lake City, Utah was of much help with the historical data that was needed.

Ray Merrick of Aurora, Colorado, is a former vice-president of the Western Outlaw-Lawman Association, whom this author met at a convention in Denver, Colorado. It was at this time he gave me the story I have included in this book. Many Thanks.

The Montezuma Valley Journal of Cortez, Colorado should be commended for its reliable and accurate reporting in 1935 and again in 1939. Its news stories were of great benefit to this author. A great big bundle of thanks. Many thanks to the *Montrose Daily Press* of Montrose, Colorado. Thank you for you great copy and making it so readily available for researchers doing historical work.

My heartfelt thanks and gratitude to my friend Jack Bailey. He has been a reservoir of cowboy lore and early history. He will celebrate ninety-seven years in July 1999, and he's still going strong.

Many thanks to Vere Ray, a friend of the author and a cowboy who had much to offer in story lore. He was a cousin of the McCarty boys but straight as an arrow. His memory is cherished.

An almost forgotten phone call from Bob and Ann Riley of La Sal Creek, Utah has led to the recent acquaintance and blossoming friendship of the author and this wonderful couple. To merely say thanks for so much wonderful help, in so many ways, would be such an understatement. Gratitude and love are much more fitting.

Thomas Lloyd Stephens is the only living son of "Mancos Jim" Stephens. He is now living in Delta, Colorado and going on eighty-five-years of age. This author wishes to extend his heartfelt thanks and gratitude for all the material he supplied and the inspiration for me to write it into story form. His own autobiography is combined with the biography of his father to make a most interesting story. Lorelei Sutherland is the daughter of Tom Stephens and is now living near Montrose, Colorado. The author extends deeply felt thanks for the photo contributions and extensive help in generating the original material.

Finally I would direct the reader to my other books, *The Mind of a Fox*, *We Shall Fall as the Leaves*, *The Hell That Was Paradox* and *In the Company of Cowboys* for further information and good reading about the real wild West.

Index

Addington, John M. Reporter, 88-89
Adsit, Harry B., 125-126
Albert, Father — Catholic Priest, 109
Aligier, Mr. & Mrs. John, 69
Andrews, Bruce — Deputy, 96
Angell, Charles — Dog handler, 79
Arizuma, Lee — Sheepman, 83
Agua — Torres Ranch, 37
Allison, Clay, 9
Animas City, 13
Armstrong, Fred, 22
A&P Railroad, 10
Aztec Cattle & Land Co., 9-10

Bailey, Jack, 163-164
Ballard, Lem — Game Warden, 72
Barrett, Fern, 99
"Beau & Bess" — Pair of Bloodhounds, 79
Bell, Carl, 43
Bell, Ida, 44
Best, Roy — Warden, 66, 108, 110
Blair, Dr., 159
Blevins, Sam Houston, 13
"Blue Lucy", 32, 44
Bothwell, Lawrence — Defense Attorney, 104, 106
Bower, Grace, 17
Brown, Neal — Sheriff Park County, 96
Broadhead, Ida, 17
Burnell, Sergeant — Aircraft Observer, 79
"Bully The" — Navajo Outlaw, 19

Campbell, Ivan, 136, 140, 143
Carey, Orin — Rancher, Guffy, Colo., 95-96
Carpenter, S.W. — Attorney, 102
Cassidy, "Butch", 115, 126, 129-131
Cassidy, Mike, 114
Carlisle Cattle Co., 22
Carr — A Gambler, 11-12
Catlin & Catlin — Law firm, 157
Caviness, Jim, 14-15
"Chief" — A blood-hound, 79, 87
Continental Cattle & Land Co., 8
Columbine Bar, 54
Cook Liquor Store, 31
Cook, Tally B. — New Mexico Sheriff, 86
"Cowboy Heaven" Song, 10

Cramer — Married Minnie Exon, 17, 24
"Crop" - Hash Knife gambler, 9, 12
Cuthbert, Mrs., 75

Daniels, John, 164
Davis, Cliff, 157-158
Dean, Frank Lynn — Mancos Deputy Marshall, 47, 58-61, 66
Decker, Chief Police Grand Junction, 98, 104-105
Delameter, Charles Eamont, 17
Dix, Katorce, 16
Dobler, Fred, 157-160
Dolores, Colorado, 20
Downey, John J. — Attorney, 102
Duncan, Lem — Cortez Deputy Sheriff, 73, 75, 91, 99-101, 105
Dunham, Irving (Honey), 149, 151-153
Dunham, Jack (John — Johnnie), 149-151
Dunham, Lena, 149-151
Dunham, Laura May, 151
Dunlap, Wesley W. — murdered sheriff, 30, 61, 74, 83, 91, 97, 99
Dunning, J. G. — County Assessor, 71
Durango, Colorado, 13, 104

Elliott, Jack, 115
Ertel, J. W. — Coroner, 57, 69
Exon, Erin, 39
Exon, Henry, 46
Exon, Jeorge, 17
Exon, John, 17
Exon, Josephine Amanda, 17
Exon, Mary Elizabeth, 17
Exon, Minnie, 17
Exon, Salmon (Sol) Samile, 17
Exon, Sarah Anne, 17
Exon Pool Hall — Mancos, 54
Exon, Somrial, 16
Exon, William James, 16, 18, 20, 39
Exon, William James II, 17

Fairlamb, Charles — Assistant District Attorney, 98
Filey, Jas. — Juror, 70
Flagstaff, Arizona, 10
Frink, Charles, 22

Geisler, George, 46
George, Jim — Marshall, 31

Index

Goldberg, Dr. George — Norwood CCC Camp, 76-77
Gold King Mine, 34-35
Graham, Tom, 12
Greager, Dewey — Kept Bloodhound "Chief", 79
Greager, Howard E. — Author, 166-167
Grimes, Gene — "Sew 'Um Up" Mesa Cattle Rustler, 121-122
Gunn, Bill — Ute Chief, 38-39

Hadden, Clarence, 44
Hallar, Fred, 15
Hamblin, Paul — Alias for Otis McDaniels, 97
Harrison, G. K. — Juror, 70
Harvey — Salesman, 89
Haywood, W. F. — Grand Junction District Attorney, 97, 99-101, 103, 105
Hash Knife Outfit, 8-11
Hatfield, Deputy District Attorney, 56
Hendrickson, Mrs. — Rock Creek Resident, 121
Henry, Jim — Navajo Police, 86
Hepworth Brothers, 22
Herman, Burl — Sheepman, 91
Hess, Joseph — Nucla Deputy, 82
Hickman, C.R. — Juror, 70
Holmes, Dr. R E — Prison Director, 110
Holbrook, Arizona, 8
Hotchkiss, John V. — Brand Inspector, 13
Hotchkiss, Uri — Rancher, 94
Houghton, Lieutenant — Air National Guard, 79
Hughes, Dan — Attorney, 159

Irvine, Charley, 158-159

Johannison, Fritz, 152-153
Johnson, Edwin C. — Governor of Colorado, 77, 101-102, 108
Johnson, E. E. — Coroner, 69

Kelsey, Presley — New Mexico Police, 86
Kent, Doctor — Kent, Texas, 5
Kratz, Frank, 54-55
Kuhre, T. P. — Juror, 70

Lewis, Ed, 44
Lockhart, Sheriff — Delta County, 94
Logan, Straud M. — District Judge, 104-106
Lone Cone Mountain, 80
Lumley, Sheriff — Mesa County, 100, 104-105

"Mancos Jim" — Paiute Chief, 21
Mancos Jim Stephens, 4, 12, 20, 24, 40, 46, 58, 66
Mathews, Owen C. — Sheriff New Mexico, 85-86
McAnally, Mac — Sheriff Montrose County, 77, 82-83, 90, 104, 107
McCarty, Bill, 117-118, 120, 122-123, 125
McCarty, Ekky, 119, 123-124
McCarty, Fred, 119-121
McCarty, George, 122-123
McCarty, Tom, 113, 118, 120, 122-123, 125
McDaniels, Herbert, 71, 87, 90, 98, 104, 106
McDaniels, Otis, 71, 87, 90, 98, 106, 108, 110
McGregor, Fred, 50, 54, 56-59
McGooch, John, 14-15
McKelvey, Franklin, 60
Medford, Fred, 102
Megaliard, Elliot, 24, 34
Menafee, Maggie, 83
Merrick, Mr. Asa — Father of Ray, 137, 141-142
Merrick, Ethel, 137, 141
Merrick, Ray, 137, 141, 143, 145
Mogollon Rim, 10
Molas Pass, 31
Monyhan, Charles J., 53
Montrose, Colorado, 37
Moore, Jerry, 62
Morefield Wel l — Ranch, 37

Naff, Miles, 165
Nash, Earl, 150
Nash, James (Jim), 149-153
Nash, Tennie, 151
Neal, C.R. — Juror, 70
Noland, James — District Attorney, 60, 83, 101, 103
Norton, Taylor, 22, 42
Nunn, L.L. — Bank President Telluride, 127

Index

O'Fallon, Owen — Rancher, 94
Offil, Arriola — Professor, 72
O'Rourke, J.B. — District Judge, 102-103, 107
Owens, Comodore — Sheriff, 13

Parker, Robert Leroy "Bud", 114-115
Parker, Katie Doramer, 17
Perkins, Rexford, 153
"Pete" — A Mule, 42, 44
Porter, E.S. — Juror, 70
Posey, Bill, 22
Posey, Paiute Chief, 19
Pratter Place, 35, 38
Pritchard, Raymond — Shepherd, 83-84

Ray, Vere, 123-124
Richener, Jack, 35
Roberts, Bob — New Mexico Deputy, 86
Robinson, Jess — Sheriff, 61, 82-83, 98, 100, 102
Rowe, Gene — Guffy, Colorado Cowboy, 95-96
Ruffe, Glenn, 76-78
"Rummy Kid", 45
Rush, Martin, 17-18

San Luis Valley, 13
Sawagerie — Posey's Paiute name, 22
Schaller, Father — Catholic Priest, 66, 110
Schofield Pass, 14
Selack, Ella, 24, 27, 34
Sharp, Fred, 150
Sharp, Hank, 11-12
Shields, Rev. Paul, 71
Silverton, Colorado, 31
Simpson, Ray — Shot two bank robbers, 121
Skinner, Jim, 157
Stevens, Frank, 22, 24
Stockton Gang, 9
Stone, Jed, 11-12
Sunnyside Mine, 23
Stephens, Albert, 20, 37, 53, 55
Stephens, Amanda Josephine Exon, 5, 20, 23
Stephens, Catherine, 20
Stephens, Ely Hiram — Father of Mancos Jim, 5

Stephens, Eva, 20
Stephens, Francis, 20, 24, 38, 53
Stephens, James — Son of Mancos Jim, 20, 44, 46
Stephens, James F. — Mancos Jim, 5, 17
Stephens, Nancy Catherine Sargent — Mother, 5
Stephens, Thomas Lloyd, 5, 20-21, 23, 25, 31, 37, 42, 46, 57, 61, 64, 66
Stephens, Walter, 20, 37
Stephens, William, 5, 37
"Suzy" — Race Mare of Tom McCarty, 114
"Suzy" — White gelding of Tom McCarty, 119, 121

Taylor, Fred, 22
Teague, Arthur, 27
Teague, Clarence "Tuffy", 24, 27, 38
Teague, Scott, 40, 43
Tewksbury Clan, 12
Tonto Basin, 11
Tripp, L.E. — Justice of the Peace, 71-72

Vaught, Clyde, 74
Vaughn, R. J. Clerk — Navajo Council, 86-87

Warner, Matt, 114
Warrick, Guy — San Miguel County Sheriff, 77-78, 81, 84, 98, 100-101, 107
Weaver, Frank, 86, 102, 105
Weber, George, 30
West, Fred — Deputy, 102
Westfall, James, 69-70, 97, 102-103, 105, 109
Westfall J. T — Nephew of James, 70
Wetherills, 17-18
Williams, Bob — Alias for Herb McDaniels, 97
Williams, Emerson, 124
Williams, Frank — Sheepherder, 84, 88, 90-91
Winslow, Arizona, 10
Wolf Creek Pass, 13
Wood, David, 14
Wood, John W., 157-160
Woods, Jess — Sheriff Ouray County, 77, 90, 104

Zane Gray, 11-12
Zender, Ed — Blacksmith shop, 47
Zufelt, Arthur, 72